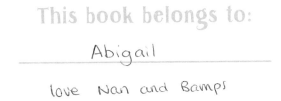

This book belongs to:

Abigail

love Nan and Bamps

A TREASURY OF
BEDTIME STORIES

Over 100 sleepytime tales and rhymes

This edition published by Parragon Books Ltd in 2017

Parragon Books Ltd
Chartist House
15–17 Trim Street
Bath BA1 1HA, UK
www.parragon.com

ISBN 978-1-4748-7085-6

Printed in China

A TREASURY OF

BEDTIME STORIES

Over 100 sleepytime tales and rhymes

PaRRagon

Bath • New York • Cologne • Melbourne • Delhi
Hong Kong • Shenzhen • Singapore

Contents

Hansel and Gretel

Once upon a time, there were two children called Hansel and Gretel. They lived in a small cottage at the edge of the forest with their father, who was a poor woodcutter, and their stepmother.

One evening, the family had nothing left to eat but a few crusts of bread. Hansel and Gretel went to bed hungry. As they lay in their beds, they heard their parents talking.

"There are too many mouths to feed," said their stepmother. "We must take the children into the thickest part of the forest and leave them there."

"Never!" cried their father.

But the next morning, Hansel and Gretel's stepmother woke them early.

"Get up!" she ordered. "We're going into the forest to chop wood."

She handed them each a crust of bread for their lunch.

With a heavy heart, the woodcutter led his children into the forest. As they walked along, Hansel secretly dropped a trail of breadcrumbs along the path.

When they reached the middle of the forest, the woodcutter said, "Wait here. We'll return at sunset."

Hansel and Gretel waited all day, but their father and stepmother didn't come back. Soon it was dark among the thick trees and Gretel was frightened.

"Don't worry," said Hansel, cuddling his sister. "We'll follow the trail of breadcrumbs I dropped along the path. It will lead us home."

But when the moon came up, they couldn't see any crumbs.

"Oh, no! The birds must have eaten them all!" whispered Hansel.

Hansel and Gretel curled up under a tree and fell fast asleep.

The next morning, they wandered through the forest until they came to a little cottage made of gingerbread and sweets!

The children were so hungry that they picked sweets off the house and crammed them into their mouths.

Just then, the door opened and an old woman hobbled out.

"Come in, children," she said, smiling. "I've got plenty more food in here."

The old woman fed them well and then put them to bed. But Hansel and Gretel didn't know that the old woman was actually a wicked witch who liked to eat children!

When Hansel and Gretel woke up, the witch grabbed Hansel and locked him in a cage. She set Gretel to work cooking huge meals to fatten up Hansel.

The weeks went by and every morning the witch went up to the cage, asking Hansel to hold out his finger.

"I want to feel if you are fat enough to eat," she said.

Hansel, being a smart boy, held out an old chicken bone instead. The witch's eyesight was so bad that she thought the bone was Hansel's finger.

One day, the witch got tired of waiting for the boy to get fatter and decided to cook him right away.

Grabbing Gretel's arm, she said, "Go and check if the oven is hot enough." And she pushed Gretel towards the open oven door. Grinning horribly, she licked her cracked lips. She was planning to eat Gretel too and couldn't wait for her delicious meal.

"I'm too big to fit in there," said Gretel, guessing the witch's wicked plan.

"You silly girl," cackled the witch. "Even I could fit in there." And she stuck her head inside. With a great big shove, Gretel pushed the witch into the oven and slammed the door shut.

"Hansel, the witch is dead!" cried Gretel, unlocking her brother's cage.

As the children made their way out of the house, they found chests crammed with gold and sparkling jewels. They filled their pockets and set off home.

Their father was overjoyed to see them. He told them that their stepmother had died while they were gone, so they had nothing to fear any more. Hansel and Gretel showed their father the treasure.

"We will never go hungry again!" he cried.

And they all lived happily ever after.

Twinkle, Twinkle, Little Star

Twinkle, twinkle, little star,
How I wonder what you are!
Up above the world so high,
Like a diamond in the sky.

When the blazing sun is gone,
When he nothing shines upon,
Then you show your little light,
Twinkle, twinkle, all the night.

Bed in Summer

In winter I get up at night,
And dress by yellow candlelight.
In summer, quite the other way,
I have to go to bed by day.

Golden Slumbers

Golden slumbers kiss your eyes,
Smiles await you when you rise.
Sleep, pretty baby, do not cry,
And I will sing a lullaby.

Bedtime

The evening is coming; the sun sinks to rest,
The rooks are all flying straight home to nest.
"Caw!' says the rook, as he flies overhead;
"It's time little people were going to bed!"

Now the Day is Over

Now the day is over,
Night is drawing nigh,
Shadows of the evening
Steal across the sky.

Now the darkness gathers,
Stars begin to peep,
Birds and beasts and flowers
Soon will be asleep.

The Butterfly Ballerina

Isabella Ballerina loved ballet. Best of all, she liked going to Madame Colette's Ballet School.

"Let us practise our ballet positions!" called Madame Colette one morning, clapping her hands. "No, no, Isabella! You are pointing the wrong foot again!"

"Sorry!" Isabella said. "I'm always getting my left and right mixed up!"

"Now, girls," cried Madame Colette. "I have exciting news to announce! We will be putting on our first show: the Butterfly Ballet. I will choose girls to play raindrop butterflies and rainbow butterflies, and one girl to dance as the sunshine butterfly!"

Back home, Isabella told Mum all about the ballet show.

"I just wish I could remember my left from my right!" she sighed.

Mum smiled. "This might help." She gave Isabella a beautiful butterfly bracelet. "Wear it on your right wrist. Then you'll always be able to tell which way is right."

At each ballet lesson, Isabella kept looking at her butterfly bracelet to make sure she turned the right way!

Finally, after many rehearsals, Madame Colette gave the girls their roles.

"Isabella, you will play the sunshine butterfly. Because you twirl so beautifully, you will dance the final pirouette!" said Madame Colette.

Isabella smiled. She just hoped she would turn the right way!

The week before the show, Isabella practised her pirouettes everywhere! She twirled in the garden…in her bedroom… and at the park.

On the night of the big show, all the girls dressed in tutus and shimmering butterfly wings. The lights dimmed. Beautiful music filled the room. The ballet was about to begin!

The raindrop and rainbow butterflies danced gracefully from flower to flower.

At last, it was Isabella's turn to dance. Nervously, she touched her butterfly bracelet. Then, taking a deep breath, she twirled the most perfect pirouette she had ever twirled!

The girls joined Isabella on stage and they all curtsied.

"Oops!" giggled Isabella. She had curtsied with the wrong foot forward, but it didn't matter one little bit. She would always be Isabella, Butterfly Ballerina!

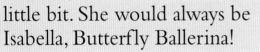

The Town and the Country Mouse

Once there were two little mice. One lived in the town, and the other in the country.

One day, Town Mouse visited Country Mouse's home. It was small and dark – not at all like Town Mouse's home.

After lunch, the two friends went for a walk. First, they strolled into a field.

"Moo!"

"What was that?" asked Town Mouse nervously.

"Just a cow," replied his friend.

So they carried on walking towards a peaceful pond.

"Hiss!"

"What was that?" asked Town Mouse, quivering from nose to tail.

"Just a goose," replied his friend.

So the two mice strolled on into a shady wood.

"Twit-twoo!"

"What was that?" yelped Town Mouse.

"An owl!" cried Country Mouse. "Quick! Run before it eats you!"

So they ran until they found a hedge to hide in.

"I don't like the country!" Town Mouse cried. "Come with me to the town. It's much better!" So they went.

Town Mouse's home was huge and grand – not at all like Country Mouse's home.

After dinner, the friends went for a walk, passing some shops on the way.

"Beep-beep!"

"What's that?" asked Country Mouse fearfully.

"Just a car," said his friend.

The mice carried on, strolling down a wide road.

"Nee-nah! Nee-nah!"

"What's that?" asked Country Mouse, his whiskers twitching.

"Just a fire engine," his friend replied.

As they pitter-pattered home, they passed a pretty garden.

"Meow!"

"What's that?" squeaked Country Mouse.

"A cat!" cried Town Mouse. "Quick! Run before it eats you!"

So they ran all the way back to Town Mouse's house.

"I don't like the town! I'm going home," cried Country Mouse.

"But what about that owl?" asked Town Mouse.

"It doesn't scare me!" cried Country Mouse. "What about that cat?"

"It doesn't scare me!" cried Town Mouse.

The two mice knew they would never agree. So they shook hands and went their separate ways.

And they lived happily ever after, each in his own way.

No One Like You

Ruff was hungry. A huge grumble rumbled around his tummy. He could hear Mum in the kitchen, and a delicious smell of freshly baked cupcakes sailed past his nose.

"Yummy," thought Ruff, and skipped into the kitchen – Mum was tidying up.

"Would you like some help?" asked Ruff. "I could try one of those cupcakes for you."

"Oh, really," said Mum, smiling.

"No one makes cakes like you," said Ruff.

Ruff was bored. He twiddled his fingers, tapped his toes, and twiddled his fingers again. He had no one to play with.

Later, Ruff tiptoed back into the living room – Mum was reading.

"Would you like something better to read?" asked Ruff. "I could find you an exciting story."

"Oh, really," said Mum, smiling.

"No one tells a story like you," said Ruff.

Ruff was annoyed. He was trying to make a model car, but he couldn't put it together. Then he had an idea!

He galloped into the garden – Mum was digging.

"Would you like something fun to do?" asked Ruff. "I could let you help me with my model."

"Oh, really," said Mum, smiling.

"No one is as much fun as you," said Ruff.

It was bedtime! Mum tucked Ruff into bed.

Ruff was feeling scared. He didn't like the shadows that flickered all around – it was very quiet. Then he had an idea.

Ruff crept out of his bedroom and into Mum's to wake Mum.

"Would you like someone to cuddle?" asked Ruff. "I'm very good at cuddling."

"Oh, really," said Mum, smiling.

"No one cuddles like you," yawned Ruff, climbing into Mum's bed.

"Oh, really," said Mum… "Well, no one loves you as much as I do. Because there is no one like you!"

Curious Kitten

Misty was a curious kitten. One day, she was watching Mrs Duck lead her waddling ducklings across the yard.

"I wonder what it's like being a duck," she thought.

She scurried along behind the ducklings, trying her best to quack, but all she could manage was a strange "Meow-ack!"

When the ducklings nibbled the grass on the riverbank, Misty tried a little herself, but it made her cough.

Then, the ducklings followed their mother into the lake for a swim.

"That looks easy," cried Misty, and she jumped in with a big SPLASH! But swimming wasn't at all easy for a kitten!

Luckily, Scratch the sheepdog was nearby. He leaped in and gently pulled Misty out, using his teeth on the scruff of her neck.

"Thanks," said Misty. "I thought it would be fun to be a duck, but I think I'll stick to being a kitten."

She had just sat down to lick her fur dry when she had an idea – perhaps she could try being a sheepdog instead!

Nippy Snippy

Eeeny, meeny, miney, mo,
Here comes Crab to pinch your toe!
Shout out loud and he'll let go –
Eeeny, meeny, miney, mo!

Nippy, snippy, snappy, snip,
Be careful when you take a dip,
Or Crab will catch you in his grip!
Nippy, snippy, snappy, snip!

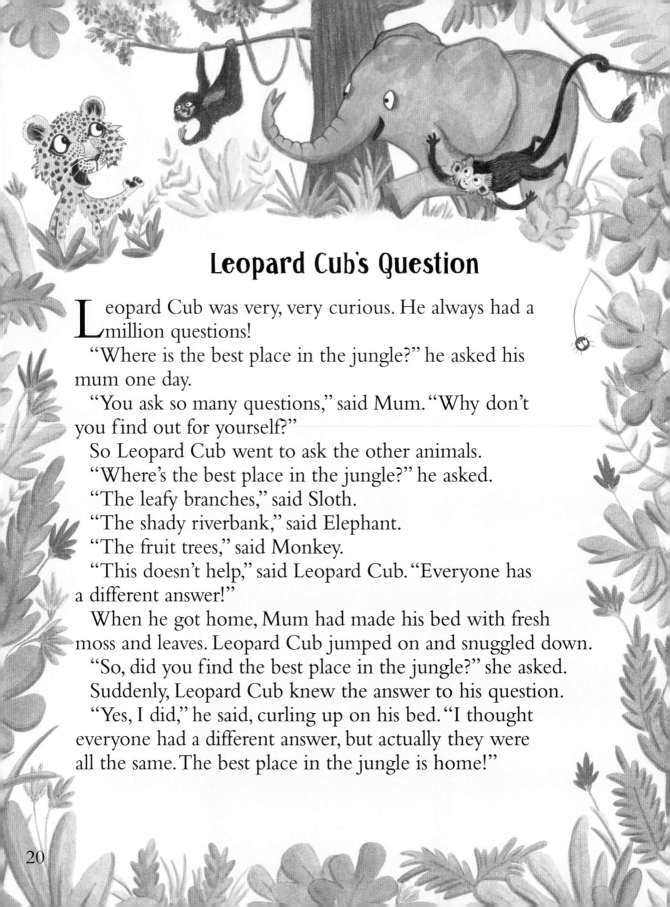

Leopard Cub's Question

Leopard Cub was very, very curious. He always had a million questions!

"Where is the best place in the jungle?" he asked his mum one day.

"You ask so many questions," said Mum. "Why don't you find out for yourself?"

So Leopard Cub went to ask the other animals.

"Where's the best place in the jungle?" he asked.

"The leafy branches," said Sloth.

"The shady riverbank," said Elephant.

"The fruit trees," said Monkey.

"This doesn't help," said Leopard Cub. "Everyone has a different answer!"

When he got home, Mum had made his bed with fresh moss and leaves. Leopard Cub jumped on and snuggled down.

"So, did you find the best place in the jungle?" she asked.

Suddenly, Leopard Cub knew the answer to his question.

"Yes, I did," he said, curling up on his bed. "I thought everyone had a different answer, but actually they were all the same. The best place in the jungle is home!"

Crocodiles Don't Wear Pyjamas

There was just one thing that Christopher Crocodile wanted – a pair of pyjamas.

"Crocodiles don't wear pyjamas," said his father. "We're too tough and scaly and scary."

But Christopher had seen a little boy wearing them once and he had never forgotten.

"Try making some yourself," suggested his mother.

So Christopher gathered large, colourful leaves and star-shaped flowers, and made the most magnificent pair of starry pyjamas.

"You look fantastic!" said his mother.

"Fabulous!" said his friends.

All the crocodiles in the swamp started asking for a pair of Christopher's pyjamas. He made more…and more…and more!

Nowadays, when the sun is shining, crocodiles look just as tough and scaly and scary as ever. But when the moon comes out and it's time for bed, every single one pulls on a wonderful pair of pyjamas.

Even Christopher's father!

The Party Zoo

Every evening, the zookeeper closed up the zoo for the night and went to bed in his zookeeper's hut. And every night there was peace and quiet in the zoo…except tonight.

"Let's have a party!" said Monkey, just as the zookeeper had gone to bed.

All the other animals thought it was a wonderful idea.

"There's a lot to organize!" said Monkey, feeling excited.

Everyone had an important job to do. The baboon band practised their music, and the penguins made iced drinks. At last, the party could begin. And WHAT a party it was!

The penguins and the dolphins had a belly-flop competition and drenched the leopards next door. Monkey fired party poppers as he swung through the trees, and the giraffe danced to the baboon band's music. The music got louder…and louder… and louder…until it woke the zookeeper up!

He peered out of his bedroom window – and couldn't believe his eyes. The ostrich was doing the hokey-cokey with the hippo, and the tigers and the lions were playing pass the parcel.

"I must be dreaming!" said the zookeeper. "It's a very good dream – I hope I don't wake up!"

Then he hurried back to bed as fast as he could.

In the morning, the zoo was very quiet. All the animals were still asleep after the party. The zookeeper thought about his dream as he swept the paths, and then he saw something lying under the tree where Monkey was going to sleep. It was a party popper!

"If I didn't know better, I'd think my dream was real!" chuckled the zookeeper.

And as he drifted off to sleep, Monkey smiled a mischievous little smile.

23

The Swallow and the Crow

One day, a young swallow landed on a branch next to a wise old crow. The swallow looked down his beak at the crow and said, "I don't think much of your stiff feathers. You should take more pride in your appearance."

The old crow was very angry and was about to fly away, when the swallow continued, "Look at me with my soft, downy feathers. They are what a well-dressed bird needs."

"Those soft feathers of yours might be all right in the spring and summer," the crow replied. "But in the winter you have to fly away to warmer countries. In the winter the trees are covered in ripe berries. I can stay here and enjoy them as I have my stiff, black feathers to keep me warm and dry."

The crow held out his wings. "What use are your fancy feathers then, Swallow?" he asked, before turning away.

And the moral of the story is: fine-weather friends are not worth much.

The Dog and His Reflection

A hungry dog passed a butcher's shop and spotted a juicy steak lying on the counter. He waited until the butcher went to the back of the shop, then he ran in and stole it.

On his way home, the dog crossed a narrow bridge over a river. As he looked down into the water he saw another dog looking up at him. This dog was also carrying a piece of meat, and it looked even bigger than the one he had!

"I want that steak too," thought the greedy dog. So he jumped into the river to steal the steak from the other dog.

But as he opened his mouth to snatch the steak, the butcher's steak fell from his mouth and sank to the bottom of the river. The other dog vanished in a pool of ripples.

The greedy dog had been fooled by his own reflection, and now he was still hungry and had nothing left to eat!

And the moral of the story is: it doesn't pay to be greedy.

Silly Billy

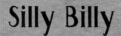

Bats do a lot of things upside down. They eat upside down. They sleep upside down. But Billy Bat spent so much time upside down that he thought up WAS down!

One night, Billy saw the reflection of the moon in the lake as he hung from his perch.

"I want to fly to the moon," he said.

"Don't be silly, Billy," said his sister, Grace. "The moon is too far away."

"No, it's not," said Billy, pointing to the reflection. "It's really close – look!"

Grace shook her head. "You don't understand!" she said.

But Billy wasn't listening.

"Here I go!" he cried. "Wheeee!" He spread his wings and zoomed towards the reflection of the moon in the water. SPLASH! Billy dived into the lake. A few seconds later, he crawled out, spluttering, and found his sister waiting for him.

"Do you understand now, Billy?" Grace asked.

"Yes," said Billy, shivering. "The moon is much, much wetter than it looks!"

What a silly Billy!

Counting Stars

Tomorrow was to be Little Panda's first day at school and she was very excited. Daddy tucked her up in bed, but she was too wide awake to close her eyes.

"I wonder what new friends I'll meet," she said. "I can't wait to find my desk and meet my teacher. School is going to be so much fun!"

Daddy tried to make Little Panda feel sleepy. He read stories, he sang lullabies and he stroked her soft fur, but she was still wide awake.

"All right," he said. "Whatever you do, don't go to sleep. You must stay awake until you have counted every single star in the sky."

The sky was crowded with twinkling stars. Little Panda started to count them.

"One…two…three…four…"

Before she even reached number ten, Little Panda's eyelids had drooped and she'd fallen fast asleep.

And what did she dream about? Her first day at school, of course!

The Princess and the Pea

Once upon a time, there lived a handsome prince. He had loving parents and plenty of friends, and lived a wonderful life in his castle. But one thing made him sad. He did not have a wife.

The prince had always wanted to marry a princess. But he wanted her to be clever and funny, and loving and kind. Not one of the princesses that he met at parties and balls was quite right.

Some of the princesses were too mean; some were too rude.

Some were too quiet; some were too loud.

And some were just plain boring!

So the prince decided to travel the world in the hope of finding a perfect princess. He met many more princesses who tried to impress him with their beauty, their dancing and their baking…but still none was quite right.

"I'm never going to meet the girl of my dreams," he sighed to himself.

"Cheer up, son," said the king. "You are still young. One day you will meet a wonderful girl, just like I met your mother."

Several months later, when even the king and queen had begun to give up hope of their son ever finding a bride, there was a terrible storm. Suddenly, there was a loud knock on the castle door.

"I wonder who could be out on such a terrible stormy night?" said the prince. When he opened the door, a pretty young girl stared back at him. She was soaked from head to toe.

"Please may I come in for a moment?" she pleaded. "I was travelling to see some friends, but I got lost in this storm, and now I am very cold and wet."

"You poor thing," said the queen. "You must stay the night. You cannot travel on in this weather."

The prince smiled at the girl. "What is your name?"

"I'm Princess Penelope," she replied. "You are all very kind. I don't want to be a bother to you."

At the word 'princess', the queen smiled to herself. She took the girl's hand and said, "Of course not. Let's get you warm and dry."

Later, the prince listened contentedly as the charming princess chatted away over supper. She was clever and funny, and loving and kind. By the end of the evening, he'd fallen in love!

The queen was delighted when she saw what was happening, but she wanted to be quite sure that Penelope was a real princess.

She went to the guest room in the castle and placed a tiny pea under the mattress. Then she told the servants to pile twenty more mattresses onto the bed and twenty feather quilts on top of the twenty mattresses!

The queen showed the princess to her room. "Sleep well, my dear," she said.

In the morning, the queen asked Penelope how she'd slept.

Penelope didn't want to be rude, but she couldn't lie. "I'm afraid I hardly slept a wink!" she replied.

"I'm so sorry," replied the queen. "Was the bed not comfortable?"

"There were so many lovely mattresses and quilts, it should have been very comfortable," replied the princess, "but I could feel something lumpy, and now I am black and blue all over!"

The queen grinned and hugged the girl to her. "That proves it!" she cried. "Only a real princess would be able to feel a tiny pea through twenty mattresses and twenty feather quilts!"

The prince was filled with joy. He had finally met the princess of his dreams! Not long after that, the prince asked Princess Penelope to be his wife. They married and the prince was never unhappy again. And as for the pea? It was put in the royal museum as proof that perfect princesses do exist!

31

You're a Big Sister

You're going to be a big sister!
And that's so lucky for you…
Babies LOVE their big sisters
And the clever things that they do.

Big sisters know babies like quiet,
So just smile and whisper, "Hello."
Big sisters are really good helpers.
Let's all get ready…and go!

All babies are cute…fun…and cuddly,
But there are things a big sister soon knows…
Babies dribble…kick…
And might even be sick…
All over your clothes and your toes!

Though they are so very tiny,
Babies can make a BIG STINK…
And when they're not feeling well…
Babies scream…and yell…
So loud you can't hear yourself think!

Babies haven't learned to play fair yet.
But remember, you were little once too!
So be kind and share…
Cuddle, play and take care…
And help them be clever like you!

When Mummy and Daddy are busy,
Always know that they love you too…
And now that you're a big sister,
Enjoy sharing with somebody new!

Elsie's Playhouse

One hot summer's day, Elsie found her dad snoozing in his garden chair.

"Dad," she called out. "I'd really like a playhouse in the garden. Will you build me one?"

"Of course, Elsie, anything you like," Dad replied, dozily. Then he turned over and fell straight back to sleep.

Elsie smiled and skipped happily away. She couldn't wait to play in her new playhouse!

"Is the playhouse finished, Dad?" Elsie asked an hour later.

Dad was still lying in his garden chair. "Elsie, making a playhouse is not as easy as all that!" he explained. "First, we'll have to draw a plan, and then…"

"That's OK, Dad. I know exactly how I want it," said Elsie. "Look, I've drawn a picture."

Elsie's playhouse had pink walls, four little windows and a bright red front door.

"Oh, I see," sighed Dad, "but I'll have to find some wood first…"

"That's okay, Dad," giggled Elsie. "There are pieces of wood in the shed."

After an hour, they had collected enough wood to make the playhouse. Dad was very hot, dusty and covered in cobwebs.

"So, can you start building it now, Dad?" asked Elsie.

"Ah, well, um, I'll need to find my tools…" groaned Dad.

"Don't worry, Dad, I've found them for you," grinned Elsie, giving him the toolbox.

Dad laughed. "Thank you. I suppose I can't put this off any longer!"

So, for the rest of the afternoon, until darkness fell, Dad hammered, drilled, sawed and painted, until…he finished the playhouse. It looked just like Elsie's drawing.

"Elsie will be so pleased," thought Dad, exhausted. He couldn't wait to see the look on her face.

But when he went into the living room, Elsie was fast asleep on the sofa.

"Elsie," he called gently. "Wake up, your playhouse is finished!"

"Thanks, Dad," Elsie whispered. "I'll play in it tomorrow." And she fell straight back to sleep!

Little Sheep

Little Sheep couldn't sleep,
Not a wink, not a peep!
Tossing, turning, all night through,
What was poor Little Sheep to do?

Owl came by, old and wise,
Said, "Silly sheep, use your eyes –
You're lying in a field of sheep,
Try counting them to help you sleep!"

"Seven, four, thirteen, ten –
That's not right, I'll start again…"
Till daylight came, awake he lay
And vowed he'd learn to count next day!

Over the Hills and Far Away

When I was young and had no sense
I bought a fiddle for eighteen pence,
And the only tune that I could play
Was "Over the Hills and Far Away".

Captain Rustybeard's New Rules

Captain Rustybeard loved being a pirate…mostly. "I just wish there weren't so many rules," he grumbled, thumping the Pirate Rulebook. He didn't seem to be allowed to do any of the things he really wanted.

"I'd like a pet dog," Captain Rustybeard said one day.

"Pirates don't have dogs," said the first mate, looking astonished. "A parrot is the only pet for a pirate captain. Look in the Rulebook."

"My feet ache," said Captain Rustybeard another day. "I think I'll get myself a nice, comfy pair of slippers."

"Pirates don't wear slippers!" said the boatswain in a shocked voice. "They wear stiff leather boots. It's rule number five."

"But leather boots give me blisters," Captain Rustybeard grumbled.

One sunny afternoon, Captain Rustybeard looked down through the clear water and saw dozens of oyster shells on the seabed.

"Let's dive for pearls!" he cried.

"Pirates don't dive for pearls," said the cabin boy with a gasp. "We're supposed to rob them from other ships. Do you know the Pirate Rulebook at all?"

Captain Rustybeard flung the Rulebook down on the deck and jumped up and down on it.

"I'm tired of being told what pirates don't do!" he roared. "From now on, I'm going to decide on the rules!"

At first, the crew were worried. What if other pirates laughed at them? But after a while, they started to enjoy themselves. After all, sheepskin slippers were a lot cosier than leather boots. The Captain's pet dog knew some good tricks, and they found more pearls by diving for them than by robbing ships.

"This is the life for me!" exclaimed Captain Rustybeard, wiggling his toes in his new slippers.

Soon, every pirate on the high seas had heard about Captain Rustybeard's new rules, and can you guess what?

They all wanted to join his crew!

Not-So-Scary

Glob the monster longed to be big and scary, but he had never frightened anyone. He had never even made anyone jump.

"I'm just too nice," he thought to himself. "Monsters aren't supposed to be friendly!"

One day, at monster school, Glob saw a purple monster with yellow spots, called Murkle. Glob jumped out from behind a wall to try to scare her. ROAR!

He was pleased to see she was crying.

"Are you crying because I scared you?" asked Glob.

Murkle shook her head.

"I'm crying because I've got no one to share my sweets with," she said.

"Oh," said Glob, disappointed. "I've never tried sweets before."

Murkle held out the bag with a big monster smile.

"Try one," she said.

Together, Glob and Murkle munched up the whole bag. By the time they had finished the last one, they were best friends. They both decided never to scare anyone again.

"Sweets are delicious!" said Glob. "And I think being friendly is better than being scary."

Monster Nursery

Monster nursery is a lot like normal nursery. There are teachers and toys and books. But, of course, not everything is the same.

At monster nursery, you have to be NOISY! The teachers tell you off for walking because you're supposed to run everywhere. If you make a big mess when you eat, then you'd fit right in at monster nursery.

Every morning, the little monsters sing a special song.

"Naughty monsters just like me
Love to shout and sing!
Let's all make a dreadful mess
And jump on everything!"

Then they practise making rude noises and bouncing on cushions.

In the afternoon, the little monsters do painting, just like you. But they don't paint on paper. They paint on each other!

I'm afraid only little monsters are allowed to go to monster nursery, so you will just have to read about it here instead. Unless, of course, you're a little monster too!

Claudia's Cauldron

One evening, Claudia was playing in the garden when she found a black pot with three legs.

"That looks just like a magic cauldron," said Claudia. "I wonder if I could cast a spell."

She put some rose petals into the cauldron with some strawberries from the fruit patch and said the magic word, "ABRACADABRA!"

POUF! A large cake decorated with strawberries and sugar roses appeared in front of Claudia.

"Yum!" said Claudia, eating it all up. "What a great cauldron!"

Next, she put into the cauldron a hairbrush, a sugar cube and a slice of bread. She said the magic word and POP! A black pony appeared in the garden and started munching the grass.

"Wow," said Claudia in surprise. "I've always wanted a pony!"

She sprang into the saddle and rode around the garden three times. Then she jumped down beside the cauldron once more.

"Now for the biggest spell of all," said Claudia. "A spell to make sure that I never have to go to bed again!"

Into the cauldron she dropped a broken alarm clock, a bedtime story and a picture of a star. Then she rubbed her hands together in excitement and said the magic word, "ABRACADABRA!"

Claudia waited and waited, but nothing happened.

"I'll try it again," said Claudia, this time calling out the magic word a little louder. "ABRACADABRA!"

But still nothing happened.

"Claudia!" called her daddy from the house. "Time for bed!"

Claudia sighed, and trudged reluctantly towards the house. Even the power of magic couldn't stop bedtime from happening!

The Big Race

Lucas the sports car drove along the road next to the railway track every morning, and he always saw Maisie the train.

"Beep, beep!" he shouted each day. "I'm faster than you!"

"Choo, choo!" Maisie replied. "Oh no, you're not!"

One morning, Maisie said, "I've had enough of that cheeky car thinking he's faster than me." So when she saw Lucas, she called out, "I challenge you to a race! First one to the next station is the winner."

"You're on!" chuckled Lucas, swishing his windscreen wipers. "But I warn you, I'm sure to win!"

"We'll see about that!" said Maisie with a grin. "Ready, steady, GO!"

Maisie blew her whistle and shot into a tunnel. Lucas screeched around the bend and zoomed under a bridge. What an exciting start to the race!

Maisie was speeding along the track, but then the signal changed, and she had to stop to let another train pass. Lucas whizzed past on the road by the rail tracks.

"See you later, slowcoach!" he hooted.

When the signal changed, Maisie chuffed ahead as fast as she could, puffing and panting. Then she spotted Lucas stuck in a traffic jam on the road ahead.

"Aha!" she said. "I'm catching up after all!"

Lucas weaved through the town and Maisie rumbled along the track. They were neck and neck! Who would win?

At last Maisie pulled into the station…just as Lucas skidded up outside. It was a draw.

"That was fun!" said Maisie, laughing. "But we still haven't found out who's fastest!"

Just then they heard a loud roar overhead.

"I'm faster than both of you!" shouted Olivia the aeroplane from high up in the clouds. "Want a race?"

45

The Sorcerer's Apprentice

Once a young boy called Franz worked as an apprentice to a sorcerer.

Every day, the sorcerer gave Franz a long list of chores to do around the castle, while he disappeared into his workshop to chant spells, or journeyed to nearby villages.

But Franz wanted to learn magic! He knew the sorcerer kept a spell book in his workshop and he longed to read it. So he decided to sneak a look the next time the sorcerer went out.

One day, as the sorcerer was getting ready to leave the castle, he ordered Franz to clean the floor of the Great Hall.

"Fetch water from the well with this bucket, then carry it to the big stone container in the hall," he said. "When the container is full of water, scrub the floor with this broom."

As soon as the sorcerer left, Franz rushed to get his master's spell book. Inside, Franz saw a spell that could bring objects to life.

"The broom could clean the floor by itself!" he cried, excitedly.

As Franz chanted the spell, the broom suddenly sprouted little arms and leaped into action. It carried the bucket to the well and fetched water to fill the container.

After a while, Franz noticed that the container was overflowing. There was water all over the floor.

"Stop!" he shouted. But the broom carried on.

Panicking, Franz grabbed an axe and chopped the broom into small pieces. But the little pieces of broom grew arms too. Soon there was an army of new brooms.

The sorcerer returned just as the overflowing water reached Franz's knees.

"Please forgive me, master," Franz cried. "I just wanted to try magic."

The sorcerer was angry. He chanted a spell and in an instant the brooms all vanished and the water disappeared.

"You have much to learn," the sorcerer told Franz, sternly.

"I promise to work very hard," the apprentice replied.

"Very well," replied the sorcerer, "you can start by cleaning this floor – the old-fashioned way!"

In a Spin

I had a little teddy,
He went everywhere with me,
But now I've gone and lost him,
Oh, where can my teddy be?

I've looked behind the sofa,
I've looked beneath the bed,
I've looked out in the garden,
And in the garden shed!

I've looked inside the bathtub,
And underneath my chair,
Oh, where, oh, where is Teddy?
I've hunted everywhere!

At last I try the kitchen,
My face breaks in a grin.
There's Teddy in the washtub –
Mum's sent him for a spin!

The Egg

Little Parrot lived in a nest with Mummy and a big pink speckled egg.

"I'm going to find some food," Mummy told her one day. "You must look after the egg until I return."

Little Parrot watched the egg for a very long time.

Then she wobbled it around to make it comfortable, and wrapped her wings around it to keep it warm.

"I'm very good at looking after eggs," she squawked, feeling pleased with herself.

Just then, Little Parrot heard a tap, tap, tapping noise coming from the egg, then…CRACK!

"Oh no, I've broken it!" she cried. "Mummy will be cross!"

But when Mummy returned, she wasn't angry at all.

"Look," she said, as a tiny baby parrot popped out of the broken eggshell. "You took care of the egg perfectly. Now it's hatched and you've got a new baby sister to play with!"

Noah's Ark

Long, long ago, when the world was still new, God looked down and saw that the people on Earth had become wicked. They had forgotten that God wanted them to be good. Instead of helping each other, they spent all their time fighting and hurting one another.

All this wickedness made God unhappy.

But an old man called Noah remembered God. Noah and his family spent their days working hard and being kind to their neighbours and to each other. God was pleased with Noah and his family.

One day, God spoke to Noah.

"The world is too full of wickedness," God said, "and I am going to send a flood to destroy the Earth and everyone on it. But I will keep you and your family safe."

"What must I do?" asked Noah.

"Build a big boat called an ark," said God. "It must be big enough to hold you and your whole family, and two of every animal in the world."

Noah got to work right away. His sons, Ham, Shem and Japheth, all helped.

They planned and measured…they chopped and sawed…they hammered and heaved…and together, they built a great, strong ark.

At last the ark was ready. Noah's wife, his sons and his sons' wives all climbed aboard.

Then Noah gathered two of every animal on Earth – every creature that hopped or walked or crawled or flew came to board the ark.

There were cats and bats and rats, monkeys and donkeys, hooting owls and wolves that howled, kangaroos and kinkajous, big baboons and little raccoons – so many animals, of all sorts and shapes and sizes! The ark held them all.

When the last animal had climbed aboard, Noah went inside and shut the door of the ark. Then the rain started to fall.

It rained and rained, and the water rose higher and higher, covering everything on Earth.

Even the tops of the highest mountains were under water!

But the ark floated on the water and, inside, everyone was safe and warm and dry.

Finally, after forty days and forty nights, the rain stopped.

Then strong winds began to blow, drying up the water.

Soon the mountaintops appeared, and the ark came to rest on a mountain called Ararat.

One day Noah sent a raven out of the ark. Soon it came back – it hadn't found anywhere to land.

A week later, Noah sent a dove out.

This time it came back with an olive branch in its beak – so Noah knew that it had found some trees, and that the Earth was almost dry.

Noah waited another week, then sent the dove out again. This time the dove did not come back – it had found a place to land!

"It is time to leave the ark!" Noah told his family. He opened the doors, and all the animals went out – all the birds and beasts, and all the creeping, crawling creatures. They spread out to find homes and raise their families.

Finally, Noah and his family left the ark. They were so happy to be back on dry land!

The first thing Noah did was pray to God to say thank you for keeping him and his family safe from the flood.

Suddenly Noah saw something beautiful in the sky – a bright, shining rainbow!

"This rainbow is a sign of my promise to you, Noah," God said. "I will never again send a flood to destroy the Earth."

These days, whenever we see a rainbow in the sky, we remember Noah, and God's promise to him – and to us.

I'm a Big Brother!

Luke was very excited. Grandma and Grandpa had been looking after him, but now Mummy and Daddy were home.

And they had a wonderful surprise – a new baby!

"The baby is so tiny!" said Luke.

"You were this tiny once," said Daddy. "But now you're big – you're Baby's big brother!"

"Can I play with Baby?" Luke asked.

"Soon," said Mummy. "But right now Baby needs to sleep." She put the baby in a cot.

"I'll wait until the baby wakes up," Luke thought. "Then maybe we'll be able to play."

But the baby woke up, and was still too tiny to play with Luke!

And the baby was still too tiny to play the next day, and the day after, and the day after that!

"You need to wait just a little bit longer," Mummy said.

All Baby seemed to do was sleep or cry or eat, or need a clean nappy.

"I wish Baby would hurry up and grow!" Luke said every day.

One morning, when Luke looked into Baby's cot, Baby was smiling – and sitting up!

Luke was so excited that he called Mummy and Daddy.

"Baby's getting bigger," they told Luke.

"Big enough to play with me?" asked Luke, holding up his toy aeroplane.

"Not big enough to play aeroplanes with you," Daddy explained. "You'll have to wait a bit longer for that."

Later, Luke watched as Daddy fed the baby. "Is Baby ever going to be big enough to play with me?" Luke asked.

"Yes," said Daddy. "You were once as little as Baby, but you got big enough to play – and Baby will too!" And Baby did start to grow. Baby grew bigger…and bigger!

Luke learned how to help dress Baby and how to help feed Baby. Baby was a very messy eater!

"Baby is very lucky to have a helpful big brother like you," said Daddy.

One afternoon, Mummy said to Luke, "Let's take Baby to the park."

"Will Baby be able to play in the sandpit with me? Or come on the swings?" Luke asked.

"Not just yet," said Mummy. "But Baby would love to watch you! A big brother can show Baby all sorts of things."

At the park, Luke rushed to the sandpit. "I'll show Baby how to make a sandcastle!" he said.

Baby happily watched Luke build a wonderful sandcastle.

"It's even more fun when Baby watches," Luke said.

"I think Baby is having fun too!" said Mummy.

That night, Luke said he would like to help Mummy give Baby a bath.

While Mummy washed Baby, Luke sailed a boat through the bubbles and made little splashes in the water.

Baby laughed and kicked and splashed too. It was lots of fun – almost like playing with Baby!

A few days later, Luke was playing with his train in the living room. Suddenly, Baby crawled over and grabbed the engine!

"Mummy! Daddy!" cried Luke. "Baby is taking my train! Make Baby stop!"

"I think Baby is trying to tell you something," Mummy said.

"What?" Luke asked.

"I think," said Mummy, "that Baby is saying… 'I'm ready to play with you now!'"

"Hooray!" cried Luke. He ran to the toybox and picked up a soft, squishy ball.

"Catch!" said Luke, as he rolled the ball to Baby. Baby laughed and tried to catch the ball. Luke rolled the ball to Baby again, and this time Baby grabbed it.

Baby laughed, and Luke laughed too.

He rolled the ball to Baby again and again.
"I think," Luke said to Mummy and Daddy, "that being a big brother is going to be lots of fun from now on!"

And it was!

Go to Bed, Tom

Go to bed, Tom,
Go to bed, Tom,
Tired or not, Tom,
Go to bed, Tom.

Rock-A-Bye, Baby

Rock-a-bye, baby, on the tree top,
When the wind blows, the cradle will rock.
When the bough breaks, the cradle will fall,
Down will come baby, cradle and all.

Little Fred

When little Fred went to bed,
He always said his prayers,
He kissed Mum, and then Papa,
And straightaway went upstairs.

Bend and Stretch

Bend and stretch, reach for the stars.
There goes Jupiter, here comes Mars.
Bend and stretch, reach for the sky.
Stand on tip-e-toe, oh! So high!

Baby Bear

Brett was a baby bear cub who just couldn't wait to grow up into a big bear.

"I wish I was big and strong like Daddy," he told Mummy Bear one morning. "Then I could leave home and look after myself, just like a grown-up bear."

Mummy Bear smiled and ruffled Brett's furry little head.

"Don't be in such a hurry to grow up," she whispered. "You're my beautiful baby, and I love taking care of you."

"I'm not a baby," cried Brett. "I'm a big bear!"

And to show Mummy just how big he was, he leapt into the river and splashed around until, after a bit of a fight, he managed to catch a tiny, wriggling fish in his mouth.

"See," he cried triumphantly, proudly showing Mummy Bear what he had caught. "I can catch fish like a big grown-up bear."

"Well done," cried Mummy. Then she dipped a large paw into a pool and flipped out a huge fish.

"Oooh," gulped Brett. "I guess I've still got a bit to learn about fishing."

Mummy and Brett sat down beside the river and began to gnaw on their fish.

Suddenly, a large eagle began circling above them. He had a huge, curved beak, and razor-sharp claws.

Brett leapt to his feet and began waving his paws around wildly.

"Go away, you big brute!" he bellowed at the top of his voice. The eagle ignored him and prepared to dive.

Mummy Bear lifted up her head and gave a gentle growl. The eagle took one look at her sharp teeth and long claws and soared back up into the sky

"Oooh," gulped Brett. "I guess I've got a bit to learn about scaring eagles."

Mummy Bear smiled kindly. Then she picked up Brett and gave him a big, hairy hug.

"There's plenty of time to grow up. You should enjoy being my baby bear first."

"Yes," agreed Brett, snuggling up to his Mummy's warm, soft fur. "Being your baby is kind of nice, after all!"

Time for Bed

As dusk fell over the jungle, the elephants huddled together and prepared to sleep. But Tootles the baby elephant wasn't ready for bed. He stomped around and drew patterns with his trunk in the dust.

"Come on, Tootles," smiled Mum. "It's time for bed."

Tootles tried to hide a yawn. "Can't we stay up and play?" he asked. "I don't want to go to sleep."

"Why not?" asked Mum. "You must be tired after such a long day."

"I don't want to say," said Tootles shyly. "You'll think I'm silly."

"I could never think you were silly," said Mum kindly. "Tell me what's troubling you."

Tootles looked up at his Mum and blushed. "I don't like the dark," he admitted. "Why does it have to be dark at bedtime? It makes me feel afraid."

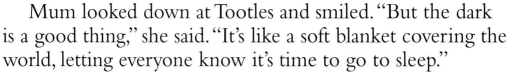

Mum looked down at Tootles and smiled. "But the dark is a good thing," she said. "It's like a soft blanket covering the world, letting everyone know it's time to go to sleep."

"But I might have bad dreams," said Tootles, who was still not convinced.

"No, you won't," said Mum. "The world is full of good dreams, if you know where to find them. Look up at the sky."

So Tootles looked up at the night sky. It was a moonlit night, and the sky was full of twinkling stars.

"Each star is a good dream, just waiting for you," explained Mum. "And just look at how many there are!"

"Wow!" said Tootles. "There must be millions. I can't wait to go to sleep now...I wonder how many good dreams I will have tonight!"

Tootles began to count the stars, but before he got to ten, he was sound asleep.

Mum smiled

down at him and wrapped her trunk around his warm body. "Sweet dreams!" she whispered.

The Owl and the Pussy Cat

The Owl and the Pussy Cat went to sea
In a beautiful pea-green boat.
They took some honey, and plenty of money,
Wrapped up in a five-pound note.

The Owl looked up to the stars above,
And sang to a small guitar,
"Oh, lovely Pussy Cat! Oh, Pussy Cat, my love,
What a beautiful Pussy Cat you are, you are,
What a beautiful Pussy Cat you are."

Pussy Cat said to the Owl, "You elegant fowl,
How charmingly sweet you sing.
Oh, let us be married, too long we have tarried.
But what shall we do for a ring?"

They sailed away, for a year and a day,
To the land where the Bong-tree grows,
And there in a wood a Piggy-wig stood
With a ring at the end of his nose, his nose, his nose,
With a ring at the end of his nose.

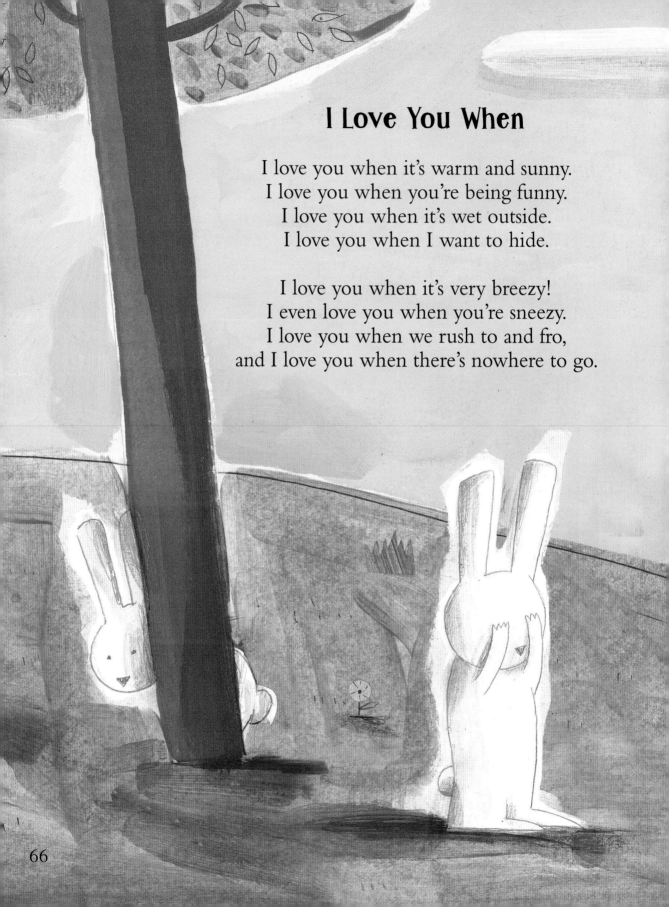

I Love You When

I love you when it's warm and sunny.
I love you when you're being funny.
I love you when it's wet outside.
I love you when I want to hide.

I love you when it's very breezy!
I even love you when you're sneezy.
I love you when we rush to and fro,
and I love you when there's nowhere to go.

I love you when you're feeling sleepy.
I love you when you're sad and weepy.
I love you when you giggle…
when you wiggle…
when you wriggle…

I love you when you're snuggly.
I love you when you're huggly.
I love you when you say, "I love you too."
But mostly I love you whenever I'm with you.

The Moonlight Tooth Fairy

Twinkle was a tooth fairy. Every night, she flew from house to house collecting the teeth that children had left under their pillows.

Each time she took a tooth, she slipped a shiny coin in its place. Twinkle loved to make people happy, but she often felt lonely.

"I wish I had a friend," she thought.

One night, Twinkle came to Isla's house. As she flew through the open window, she felt somebody watching her. A fairy face stared at her in the moonlight. And another. There were fairy pictures and toys everywhere!

Twinkle was so surprised, she dropped the coin. The noise woke Isla.

Isla gasped when she spotted Twinkle.

Twinkle started to cry. "You've seen me! I've broken the most important fairy rule!"

"Don't cry!" said Isla, gazing at Twinkle in amazement. "I won't tell anyone, I promise."

"And I've lost your coin!" sobbed Twinkle.

Isla had an idea. "Instead of giving me a coin, could you grant me a fairy wish?" she asked.

"What would you wish for?" said Twinkle, drying her tears.

"I wish to be a fairy just like you!"

Twinkle waved magic into the room.

Suddenly, Isla felt herself shrinking.

"I'm growing wings!" she cried with joy. "Will you teach me how to fly?"

"It's easy!" said Twinkle. "Hold my hand…"

Twinkle led Isla out into the moonlit garden. They flew between the trees and skimmed a starry pond.

"I love being a fairy!" cried Isla.

"It's much more fun with two," laughed Twinkle happily. At last she had a real friend of her own.

Soon, it was time for Isla to go back to being a little girl. "Thank you for making my wish come true," she said to Twinkle.

"You've made my wish come true, too!" replied Twinkle.

Twinkle promised to come back soon.

As she flew away, she whispered, "Sweet dreams, my fairy friend!"

The Best Easter Egg Hunt Ever

On a warm spring day, in the tall green grass, a little grey rabbit was sniffing the air.

It was Easter Day. It was egg-hunt time.

Mother Rabbit said, "There are lots of eggs to find. There are stripy eggs and spotty eggs, sky-blue eggs, pale pink eggs and eggs as bright as buttercups!"

"I want a special egg," said Rabbit. And off she hopped to see what she could find.

Down in the farmyard, Chick was hopping round a haystack.

"Please help me, Rabbit," he cheeped. "I can't reach that egg."

Rabbit hopped onto the haystack in one leap. Nestled in the hay was a sky-blue Easter egg.

"I haven't got much," said Chick. "But I can give you some feathers to say thank you."

Rabbit tucked the feathers into her basket and off she hopped.

The flowers waved in the breeze and the air was full of bees. Rabbit hopped with happiness. She followed a fluttering butterfly and nibbled a yellow-green leaf. She picked a bunch of spring flowers.

"Oh," Rabbit laughed. "I almost forgot about finding an egg. And off she hopped…

Rabbit looked for an egg among the tree trunks and in the hedgerows. She found some scraps of sheep's wool stuck in the brambles, but she didn't find a single egg. So off she hopped.

In the sunlit woodland, Rabbit heard a squeak.

"I can't dig up this egg!" said Mouse.

"I'll help," said Rabbit. "I can dig."

SCRAPE. SCRATCH. DIG. BURROW.

"Wow!" breathed Mouse, looking at the giant egg. "It's bigger than our whole mouse hole!" And Mouse gave Rabbit some tasty grass to say thank you.

Rabbit's ears drooped.

"Mouse found a special egg," she sighed. "But I haven't found any."

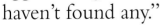

Rabbit didn't feel like hopping any more. She sat down by the duck pond.

And there, by the water's edge, was an egg. But it wasn't big or bright, spotty or stripy, pink or blue or yellow. It was small and dull and white.

"It doesn't look very special," said Rabbit.

Rabbit touched the egg with her paw. "Oh," she whispered. "It's warm!"

A cold breeze blew. Rabbit shivered.

"Don't worry, little egg," she said. "I'll keep you warm."

And Rabbit emptied out her basket. She took the stalks of grass and the sweet flowers and wove them together. She shaped a little cup. She lined it with warm wool and soft feathers. She made a nest.

And when the egg was safe and warm, Rabbit curled up close by. She was tired after her long day. Soon she was fast asleep.

Peep! Peep!

What was that noise?

Peep! Peep!

It was coming from inside the egg.

The egg wobbled and rocked in the nest, and all the time it went Peep! Peep! Peep!

Until CRICK! Out came a beak!

And CRACK! Out came…

"A duckling!"

"Quack! Quack!" Mother Duck swam to shore. "Oh, thank you!" she said. "My egg! I've been looking for it all day."

Rabbit smiled. "I'm glad I found this egg," she said. "It's the most wonderful Easter egg of all."

Why the Hippopotamus Lives in the Water

A long time ago, there was a huge hippo. Nobody except the hippo's family knew his name.

One day, the hippo asked the other animals to guess his name. But, as the hippo had suspected, no one could get it right.

"What would you do if I told you your name?" asked a little tortoise.

"I would be so ashamed that my family and I would leave the land to live in the water," replied the hippo. "We would only come out at night to feed."

Soon, after noticing that the hippo and his family washed and drank in the lake every day, the tortoise hid by a bush and waited until they were returning home.

As the hippo's wife trailed behind her family, the tortoise crept onto the path in front of her, then tucked into his shell.

"Ouch!" cried the hippo's wife, as she bumped into the tortoise's hard shell. "Isantim, my husband, I've hurt my foot!"

Later, the tortoise told the hippo his name and Isantim kept his promise. And that's why hippopotamuses live in the water.

How the Rabbit Lost His Tail

Mrs Cat was very jealous of Mr Rabbit's long tail, as she didn't have one. So Mrs Cat stole Mr Rabbit's fine tail. Then she took a needle and thread out of her basket and sewed the tail onto her own body.

"It looks so much better on me!" Mrs Cat purred happily.

"I found my tail too long, anyway," Mr Rabbit replied. "You can keep it if you give me your basket." So she did.

And Mr Rabbit hopped off into the forest with the basket.

"I've lost my tail, but I've gained a basket," he thought. "Maybe I'll find a new tail or something else just as good."

After a while, Mr Rabbit found a garden. He saw an old woman picking lettuce.

"Oh, please, Mr Rabbit," she said, "could I borrow your basket to put my lettuce in?"

"If you give me some of your lettuce," replied Mr Rabbit, "you can keep the basket!" So she did. And off he hopped.

Soon Mr Rabbit felt hungry. He took a bite of the lettuce. It was delicious!

"I've lost my tail and my basket, but I've found something I like much better!" he thought, feeling happy.

75

The Littlest Pig

L ittle Pig had a secret. He snuggled down in the warm hay
with his family and smiled a secret smile. Maybe it wasn't so
bad being the littlest pig after all…

Not so long ago, Little Pig had been feeling really fed up.
He was the smallest pig in the family. He had five brothers and
five sisters and they were all much bigger and fatter than he
was. They were very greedy and ate most of the food from the
feeding trough before Little Pig had a chance!

Then one day Little Pig had made an important discovery: a
little hole in the fence, tucked away behind the feeding trough.
He could just fit through the hole because he was so little.

He waited all day until it was time for bed, and then, when
all his family were fast asleep, he wriggled through the hole.
Suddenly he was outside, free to go wherever he pleased.
And what an adventure he had!

First, he ran to the henhouse and gobbled up the bowls of grain. Then he ran into the vegetable patch and munched a whole row of cabbages. What a wonderful feast! When his little belly was full to bursting, he headed for home.

Night after night Little Pig had tasty adventures. Sometimes he would find the farm dog's bowl filled with scraps from the farmer's supper, or come across buckets of oats ready for the horses.

As the days and weeks went by, Little Pig grew bigger and fatter. He knew that soon he would no longer be able to fit through the hole, but for now, snuggled down in the warm hay, he was enjoying his secret!

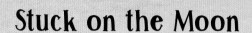

Stuck on the Moon

Every night, when the moon and the stars were out and the children had gone to bed, the pages of the nursery rhyme book started to flutter. The characters clambered out, then played and sang together.

But one night, the cow who jumped over the moon didn't jump over the moon. She got stuck! Everyone looked up at the cow, stuck on the moon.

"Oh dear," said Incy Wincy spider. "That wasn't supposed to happen."

"We have to get her down before the children wake up," said Jack Sprat. "We can't have anyone missing from the book."

Luckily, Humpty Dumpty had an idea.

"Let's stand on each other's shoulders," he said. "We can reach the moon and help the cow get down."

So one by one, they clambered onto each other's shoulders.

The three little pigs stood on the book, the crooked man stood on the three little pigs, the owl stood on the dish, and so on. It took a long time, but at last the wibbling, wobbling ladder of characters reached almost up to the shining moon. Almost…

"Who's missing?" cried Little Bo-Peep.

Suddenly, they all heard a loud crash. One of the five little monkeys had been playing with a ball of wool, and had pushed it right out of the book!

"Little monkey, come on!" they shouted. So the monkey clambered above his brothers and sisters, and all the way to the top of the swaying ladder. He helped the cow down, and then everyone ran back to their places in the book, just in time, before the children started to open their eyes!

A Drink for Blaze the Dragon

It was a very hot day and Blaze's mother was sleeping in the cool cave. But Blaze didn't want to sleep. He wanted to whizz around the mountain. He crept outside.

Wheeee! But flying around in the sizzling heat soon made Blaze thirsty. He flopped down by the lake at the bottom of the valley. Then he remembered his mother's warning.

"Dragons can ONLY drink juniper juice!" she'd told him.

Blaze watched eagerly as a flock of birds drank from the lake. He was too hot to fly all the way home for juniper juice. Surely a little water wouldn't hurt? He licked up a few drops.

"Delicious," Blaze gasped. He dipped his whole face into the lake and the cold water rushed into his mouth.

Suddenly…PFFFT! Blaze's dragon flames went out.

Blaze was terrified. He flew home as fast as he could.

"Mum," he cried. "I'm not a dragon any more. Look! My fire has gone out!"

"Did you drink the lake water?" asked his mother sternly.

"I did!" he sobbed. "I didn't listen to you."

"There's only one way to get your fire back," she sighed. "We'll have to fly to the volcano. You must swallow its heat."

The burning volcano rumbled and crackled with molten lava as Blaze and his mother flew towards it.

Shaking with fear, the young dragon swooped down as low as he dared and took in a deep, fiery breath.

Blaze landed in the valley below, coughing and spluttering. Suddenly, flickers of orange fire shot out of his nose.

"Mum, it worked – I've got my fire back!" he cried.

Blaze's mother couldn't stay cross with him any more.

"Let's go home," she laughed. "Breathing in that volcano fire must have made you thirsty…for a nice glass of juniper juice!"

Come to Bed, Says Sleepy-head

"Come to bed," says Sleepy-head.
"Tarry a while," says Slow.
"Put on the pot," says Greedy-gut,
"Let's sup before we go."

Wee Willie Winkie

Wee Willie Winkie
Runs through the town,
Upstairs and downstairs
In his nightgown.
Rapping at the window,
Crying through the lock,
"Are the children all in bed?
It's past eight o'clock."

82

Brahms' Lullaby

Lullaby, and good night,
With rosy bed light,
With lilies overspread,
Is my sweet baby's head.
Lullaby, and good night,
You're your mother's delight,
Shining angels beside
My darling abide.

Go to Sleep

Go to sleep, my baby,
Close your pretty eyes,
Angels are above us,
Peeping through the skies.
Great big moon is shining,
Stars begin to peep.
Time for little babies
All to go to sleep.

Diddle Diddle Dumpling

Diddle, diddle, dumpling, my son John,
Went to bed with his trousers on,
One shoe off, and the other shoe on,
Diddle, diddle, dumpling, my son John.

The Pink Princess

Princess Sophia loved pink. She had a bright pink room with a plump pink bed. She had a huge pink wardrobe full of frilly pink dresses. She had rosebud-pink shoes and a pink tiara.

One day, Princess Chloe came to play at the palace. She brought Princess Sophia a lovely new necklace! But there was only one problem…

"It's not pink!" cried Princess Sophia. It really was beautiful, but it wouldn't go with her pink dress, pink shoes or pink tiara!

"Let's go and play!" cried Princess Chloe.

Princess Sophia put the necklace in her pocket and followed Princess Chloe into the palace garden.

Princess Chloe ran up to the gardener, who was busy mowing the palace lawn.

"May we pick some flowers, please?" asked Princess Chloe.

When the gardener said that they could, Princess Chloe skipped away, picking different-coloured flowers as she went.

Princess Sophia noticed some bright purple blossom. She picked some of it and put it in her hair, just like Princess Chloe.

Princess Chloe started to climb a huge tree.

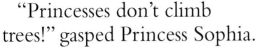

"Princesses don't climb trees!" gasped Princess Sophia.

"Why not?" said Princess Chloe. "Look, I've found some ribbons up here!"

Princess Sophia recognized the ribbons of a kite she had lost. She climbed up into the tree. Princess Chloe untangled the ribbons and tied one around each of their waists.

"Now catch me if you can!" said Princess Chloe, and she scrambled down the tree and ran to the pond.

A dragonfly fluttered past them, its shimmering wings catching the sun. It landed on Princess Chloe's outstretched hand. Princess Sophia jumped back nervously.

Princess Chloe whispered to the dragonfly, "She doesn't like anything that isn't pink."

"Yes, I do!" shouted Princess Sophia. "I like the bright flowers and the rainbow-coloured ribbons, and the blue pond and this gorgeous, multi-coloured dragonfly!"

"Why don't you try on your new necklace now?" asked Princess Chloe.

Princess Sophia admired her colourful reflection in the pond.

"I don't mind that it's not a pink necklace…" she said, smiling. "Because I'm not just a pink princess any more!"

Tia and Teddy

Tia Mouse's favourite toy was Teddy. Teddy went with Tia everywhere. When Teddy was with Tia, Tia wasn't scared of anything. She wasn't scared of climbing to the top of the stalks of corn in the field nearby, or bigger mice, or doing somersaults, or anything at all.

"You and Teddy are so brave!" Mum would say, as Tia told her about another one of their adventures together.

One afternoon, though, Tia looked all through the mouse hole, but she couldn't find Teddy anywhere.

Tia started to cry. "Mum! Teddy's gone missing!"

Mum came out of the study. "I'm sure he's somewhere, Tia," she said. "Don't worry, we'll find him."

"I'm scared without Teddy," said Tia.

Tia and Mum went to look for Teddy. They looked in the corn field. Then they looked down by the stream. And there was Teddy! He was propped up against a tree.

"We were looking at the fish this morning with Dad," said Tia. "Teddy must have decided to watch them for a bit longer."

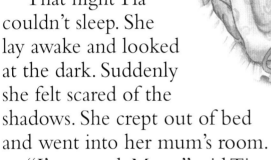

"Well he's found now," said Mum, giving them both a big hug.

That night Tia couldn't sleep. She lay awake and looked at the dark. Suddenly she felt scared of the shadows. She crept out of bed and went into her mum's room.

"I'm scared, Mum," said Tia.

"But you're never scared when you're with Teddy," said Mum.

"But what if I lose him again?" said Tia.

Mum smiled. "Let me tell you a secret," she said. "Do you know what Teddy said to me when we came back from the stream this morning? He told me that he was scared when he was on his own by the stream, but he's never scared when he's with you, because you're so brave."

"So I think Teddy's the brave one," said Tia…

"…but he thinks you are!" finished Mum.

"Perhaps we're both brave," said Tia. "Do you know, I think I might be ready to go back to bed now." She gave Mum a big hug, and Mum hugged her and Teddy back.

"Night, night, Tia. Night, night, Teddy," said Mum.

"Night, night, Mum," said Tia. "Teddy says 'night night' as well. And he says to tell you he's not scared any more."

Little Red Riding Hood

There was once a sweet little girl who always wore a lovely red cape with a hood. So everyone called her Little Red Riding Hood.

"Granny is poorly," said her mother one morning. "Take her this basket of food, and don't talk to any strangers!"

So Little Red Riding Hood took the basket and set off right away.

Very soon she met a wolf.

"Hello," said the wolf. "Where are you going?"

"I'm visiting my poorly granny," replied Little Red Riding Hood, forgetting her mother's warning. "She lives on the other side of this wood."

While Little Red Riding Hood picked some flowers for Granny, the wolf raced down the path to the old lady's cottage.

He opened the door, and before Granny had a chance to shout for help, the wicked creature opened his huge jaws and swallowed her whole! Then he climbed into her bed, pulled the covers up under his chin and waited.

Soon, Little Red Riding Hood reached Granny's house with her basket of food and posy of flowers.

When she went into the bedroom, she gasped in surprise. Her granny didn't look well at all!

"Granny," she exclaimed. "Your ears are enormous!"

"All the better to hear you with," growled the wolf.

"And your eyes are as big as saucers," she gulped.

"All the better to see you with," snarled the wolf.

"And your teeth are so…pointed!" she gasped.

"All the better to EAT you with!" roared the wolf, and he swallowed Little Red Riding Hood in one GULP! Then he fell fast asleep.

Luckily, a nearby woodcutter heard some loud snoring sounds coming from the cottage.

He tiptoed inside and found the sleeping wolf…with his tummy bulging.

So he tipped the wolf upside down and shook him hard. Out fell Little Red Riding Hood, and out fell Granny!

Granny was so furious, she chased the wolf far into the wood and they never saw him again!

Ten in the Bed

There were ten in the bed and the little one said,
"Roll over, roll over."
So they all rolled over and one fell out.

There were nine in the bed and the little one said,
"Roll over, roll over."
So they all rolled over and one fell out.

There were eight in the bed and the little one said,
"Roll over, roll over."
So they all rolled over and one fell out.

*(Repeat the rhyme, counting down from seven in the bed
to one in the bed…)*

There was one in the bed and the little one said,
"Goodnight!"

Five Little Monkeys

Five little monkeys jumping on the bed,
One fell off and bumped his head.
Mama called the Doctor and the Doctor said,
"No more monkeys jumping on the bed!"

Four little monkeys jumping on the bed,
One fell off and bumped her head.
Papa called the Doctor and the Doctor said,
"No more monkeys jumping on the bed!"

*(Repeat the rhyme, counting down from three
little monkeys to one little monkey…)*

One little monkey jumping on the bed,
He fell off and bumped his head.
Mama called the Doctor and the Doctor said,
"Put those monkeys straight to bed!"

Fairy Friends Forever

Deep in the woods, poor Eloise the fairy was trapped under a nutshell that had fallen from a tree. Try as she might, it was just too heavy for her to move.

Then, suddenly, the nutshell lifted and a little girl gazed down at her.

Eloise was scared of humans, but the girl looked kind.

"Thank you," she said. "What's your name?"

"Matilda," whispered the girl. "Are you really a fairy?"

Eloise had an idea. She waved her wand and shrank Matilda to fairy size.

"Come to Fairyland and find out!" she giggled.

Eloise showed Matilda all around her magical home. They had tea in her toadstool house and gathered dewberries in the Fairyland Forest. They giggled and shared secrets, and soon they felt as if they had always known each other.

Then, it was time for Matilda to go home. Eloise gave her a tiny Fairyland flower.

"I'll never forget you," she whispered.

"And I won't forget you," promised Matilda, as they linked their little fingers together. "Fairy friends forever!"

Winter Snowdrops

One winter's day, a fairy called Snowdrop was sitting in a tree when she heard someone crying. She fluttered down and saw a girl sitting among the tree roots.

"What's wrong, little girl?" Snowdrop asked.

"I can't find any flowers for my mother's birthday," sobbed the girl.

Snowdrop felt sorry for her.

"Fetch me the smoothest pebble you can find," she said. "Then bury it under the tree."

The little girl searched and searched, and finally found a pebble as smooth as silk. She buried it, as she'd been told, and patted the soil down. Then Snowdrop waved her wand, and tiny plant shoots poked through the soil and started to grow. They rose higher and higher, until they burst into brilliant white snowdrops.

"Thank you!" said the little girl, picking the flowers. "Mummy will love them."

The little girl never saw Snowdrop again. But every year, on the girl's mother's birthday, Snowdrop secretly used her magic, and there was always a patch of bright snowdrops waiting for the girl to pick them!

Bernie Becomes a Mum!

One day Bernie the Drake went to visit Dilly the Duck. Dilly had been sitting on her eggs for weeks and was getting bored.

"Is there anything I can do to help?" asked Bernie.

"Well, since you've asked," said Dilly, "I'd love to go for a dip in the pond. Could you keep my eggs warm while I'm gone?"

"I'd be delighted," said Bernie. "But what happens if they hatch while you are away?"

"Don't worry. They won't," laughed Dilly. "They're not due to hatch until tomorrow."

"Okay," quacked Bernie. And he settled himself gently onto the eggs and made himself comfortable.

"Ah, this is easy," thought Bernie proudly, and he began to daydream about a brood of cute ducklings calling him Uncle Bernie. He was just dozing off to sleep when a loud CRACK awoke him.

All at once, the nest was full of cracking sounds.

"What's happening?" cried Bernie, trying hard not to panic.

Bernie got up and looked beneath him. A row of fluffy faces peered back. "Mama!" quacked the little ducklings.

"I'm not your Mummy!" cried Bernie in alarm. But no matter how much he told them, the little ducklings didn't seem to hear. "Mama! Mama!" they quacked.

By the end of the morning, Bernie was at his wits' end. "I'll have to find Dilly right away!" he decided.

Bernie leaped off the nest in a flurry of feathers and raced down to the pond. "Stay there," he yelled over his shoulder. But the little ducklings were much too young to understand.

"Mama! Mama!" they quacked, as they waddled after him and plopped into the water.

Bernie didn't know what to do, so he swam round and round in circles, herding the ducklings into a neat group. He was so busy that he didn't see Dilly until she popped up beside him. He hung his head in shame. He just knew that Dilly was going to be furious. But he was wrong.

"Oh, well done, Bernie!" she quacked. "Not only have you hatched my eggs – you've taught my ducklings to swim, too! What a good mum you are."

Little Dolphin

Little Dolphin was a friendly creature who loved to visit all his ocean friends. But sometimes when he visited them it made him feel just a little bit sad.

"They are all so talented," he said to himself. "And I'm just a boring old dolphin. I wish I was more like them."

One morning, Little Dolphin met his friends for a play by the seashore. As usual, he couldn't help admiring everyone. Octopus was amazing. He could juggle urchins and tickle fish at the same time. He could even pick up seaweed with seven tentacles, while he shook hands with the eighth.

"I wish I had tentacles like you, Octopus," sighed Little Dolphin. "Then I could do lots of things at once."

Octopus blushed and told Dolphin not to be silly.

"But silly is exactly what I am," thought Little Dolphin sadly. He turned around to watch Crab.

Crab had two gigantic claws for grabbing, and lots of smaller claws for scuttling around on the sand. He could even scuttle across the seabed sideways.

"I wish I had claws like you, Crab," sighed Little Dolphin, looking at them enviously.

"Well, I don't have claws either," said Turtle, trying to make Little Dolphin feel better.

"No," said Little Dolphin. "But you do have flippers, so you can soar through the water. I can't do anything special!"

"What do you mean?" cried Turtle in surprise.

"Of course you can," added Octopus. "No one in the whole ocean can leap and do tricks like you."

Little Dolphin thought for a moment, then a smile began to spread across his face.

"You're right," he cried, leaping out of the water and performing a perfect somersault right in front of all his friends.

"Maybe being a little dolphin isn't so bad, after all," he said. "Come on everyone! Let's play!"

And that's exactly what they all did.

I Love My Mummy

One morning, Little Deer didn't want to play in his garden any more.

"I want to see new things," he told his mummy.

"Then let's go exploring," said Mummy Deer.

"This way!" cried Little Deer excitedly.

When Little Deer came to the stream, he slowly crossed the wobbly stones, watching the water as it trickled gently beside him.

"Don't get your feet wet," warned Mummy.

"I won't!" said Little Deer, as he wiggled and wobbled.

On the other side of the stream, Little Deer squeezed through the tangly bushes.

"Don't get stuck," warned Mummy.

"I won't! Hurry up, Mummy!" said Little Deer. "Look! A hill that goes up to the clouds!"

Little Deer climbed all the way to the top, panting with each step.

"I can see forever!" cried Little Deer, wobbling as he stood on tiptoes.

Then suddenly…

"Wheeee!" cried Little Deer, as he slid down the other side of the hill into a meadow.

"Are you okay?" asked his mummy.

"Yes!" giggled Little Deer. "I am!"

Little Deer looked around the meadow. "Mummy?" he said anxiously. "Which way is home? I'm lost!"

"We'll soon find our way back," Mummy Deer said soothingly. "We just have to remember how we got here."

Little Deer thought and thought. At last, he began to remember.

"We came over the hill!" said Little Deer, and he scampered back up the hill. "I can see the way from here!"

Little Deer and his mummy skidded down the other side of the hill. "We squeezed through those tangly bushes!" cried Little Deer, and they pushed through them.

"Which way now?" said Mummy Deer.

Little Deer heard the tinkling sound of a stream.

"The wobbly stones!" cheered Little Deer. "Don't get your feet wet, Mummy!"

"I won't!" laughed Mummy Deer.

Little Deer knew the way from here. He ran as fast as he could, until he reached his garden.

"I love exploring," cried Little Deer happily. "And I love my mummy!"

Little Bo-Peep

Little Bo-Peep has lost her sheep
And doesn't know where to find them.
Leave them alone
And they'll come home,
Wagging their tails behind them.

Baa, Baa, Black Sheep

Baa, baa, black sheep,
Have you any wool?
Yes sir, yes sir,
Three bags full.

One for the master,
And one for the dame,
And one for the little boy
Who lives down the lane.

Sippity Sup, Sippity Sup

Sippity sup, sippity sup,
Bread and milk from a china cup.
Bread and milk from a bright silver spoon
Made of a piece of the bright silver moon.
Sippity sup, sippity sup,
Sippity, sippity sup.

Hey Diddle Diddle

Hey diddle diddle,
The cat and the fiddle,
The cow jumped over the moon.
The little dog laughed to see such fun
And the dish ran away with the spoon!

Dance, Jiggle, Dance

The animals at Red Barn Farm were fed up. They wanted some peace and quiet but Jiggle, the donkey, was tap dancing. He was practising for the local farm dance competition. His hooves clicked and clattered loudly across the yard as he twirled, and his shrill braying could be heard for miles around as he sang along. He was determined to win. But first, he had to find a dance partner.

Jiggle clattered over to the pond to ask Duck.

"I'd like to help," quacked Duck, "but I've got flat feet."

Jiggle clopped over to the barn to ask Cow.

"I can't," mooed Cow. "If I dance about my milk gets too frothy. Why don't you ask Sheep?"

"Will you dance with me?" Jiggle asked Sheep.

"Oh, I've got such a thick coat," bleated Sheep. "I'll get too hot."

Jiggle wouldn't give up! Even though he didn't have a partner, he practised his dance moves all week.

At last, the day of the competition arrived. All the competitors gathered in the big tent, set up on the village green. Jiggle still hadn't found a dance partner, but he decided to watch Farmer Brown and Mrs Brown, who were dancing first. Everyone cheered as they made their way to the stage, but suddenly, Farmer Brown tripped and hurt his knee.

"I'm fine," he told Mrs Brown, "just carry on without me."

Mrs Brown looked around and saw Jiggle.

"Will you be my partner?" she asked. "The other animals have told me all about your dancing."

Beaming with pride, Jiggle joined Mrs Brown on the dance floor. What a pair they made, moving together in perfect rhythm!

When the judge announced that they had won first prize, it was the happiest day of Jiggle's life.

Now the other animals don't mind Jiggle's dancing quite so much. They even stop what they are doing to watch his new moves! However, if Jiggle breaks into song as he dances, the other animals just cover their ears and yell, "Please, Jiggle, just jiggle."

Moon Stars

It was bedtime. The sun was setting, the owls were swooping overhead, and the squirrels and rabbits were curling up and going to sleep. But Mummy Bear was wide awake. She couldn't find Baby Bear anywhere. He wasn't in the kitchen, eating an extra cookie. He wasn't in the bathroom, brushing his teeth. He wasn't in his bedroom, putting on his pyjamas.

"Baby Bear!" she called. "Where are you?"

But there was no reply.

Mummy Bear went out into the woods to look for him. The night animals were out and about. Freddy Bat was hanging upside down from a tree.

"Have you seen my Baby Bear?" she asked.

Freddy Bat gave a few sleepy blinks.

"No, sorry," he replied, yawning. "I've only just woken up."

Mummy Bear walked on past the babbling stream. Billy Fox was drinking some cool water.

"Have you seen my Baby Bear?" she asked.

Billy Fox looked up and shook his head.

"No, I'm afraid not," he said. "I've been eating my breakfast."

So Mummy Bear went further into the woods until she reached a little clearing. There she saw Ella Badger rolling around in the leaves.

"Have you seen my Baby Bear?" she asked.

Ella Badger thought for a moment. Then she smiled.

"I think I have," she said. "There's a fluffy little bear sitting on the top of the highest hill. I saw him when I was practising my roly-polys."

When Mummy Bear reached the highest hill, she rubbed her eyes in astonishment. Baby Bear had the moon in his lap!

"It fell out of the sky," said Baby Bear. "It landed right in my arms. How can I put it back in the sky, Mummy?"

Mummy Bear sat down next to Baby Bear and snuggled up.

"Well," she said. "Let's think. We could use sticky tape."

"Sticky tape might not be strong enough," said Baby Bear. "How about glue?"

"What if it makes the moon too messy?" said Mummy Bear. "We could bounce it back into the sky like a ball."

Baby shook his head.

"It might break instead of bouncing," he said. "I don't want to go to bed until we know what to do with the moon. How can we put it back where it belongs?"

"Let me have a look," said Mummy Bear. She sniffed the moon. She walked all the way around it. Then she smiled.

"I've got an idea," she said. "This moon looks bigger than normal. I think that it's fallen out of the sky because it grew too big and heavy, and the sky couldn't hold it up any more!"

Baby Bear opened his eyes very wide.

"How can we make it lighter?" he asked.

"Well," said Mummy Bear, "what we have to do is trim around the edges."

"What will happen then?"
asked Baby Bear.

"Let's find out," said his mummy. She took out her nail scissors and trimmed a little bit from all around the moon. Snip! Snip! Snip! And the pieces fell to the ground. Then Mummy Bear cut the pieces into star shapes to take home.

"Now," she said, "let go of the moon."

So Baby Bear did, and the moon floated back up into the sky, until it was high above their heads.

Then Mummy Bear and Baby Bear walked home.

Baby Bear climbed into bed, while Mummy Bear stuck the tiny stars all over the walls. Then she cuddled into bed beside him, and they drifted off to sleep in the golden light of the moon stars.

I Love My Daddy

One day, Little Squirrel wanted to show Daddy Squirrel all the things he could do.

"What shall we do first?" said Daddy.

"Digging!" said Little Squirrel excitedly, as he dug and dug, with his little tail wagging.

"Well done!" said Daddy. But suddenly, Little Squirrel's tail stopped wagging.

"Help, Daddy! I'm stuck!"

Daddy Squirrel helped Little Squirrel wriggle out of the hole and gave him a hug.

"You are a good digger!" said Daddy. "What shall we play next?"

"Climbing!" said Little Squirrel, and he climbed as high as he could go.

"Well done!" said Daddy. But suddenly, Little Squirrel closed his eyes tightly.

"Help, Daddy! I'm stuck!"

Daddy Squirrel helped Little Squirrel climb down and gave him a hug.

"You are a good climber!" said Daddy. "What shall we play next?"

"Jumping!" said Little Squirrel, and he jumped with a big smile on his face. But suddenly, Little Squirrel stopped smiling and…SPLAT! He was in the mud.

"Help, Daddy! I'm stuck again!"

Daddy Squirrel helped Little Squirrel out of the sticky patch of mud and gave him a hug.

"You are good at jumping!" said Daddy.

But Little Squirrel shook his head sadly.

"I can't do anything!" cried Little Squirrel. "I always get stuck!"

Daddy Squirrel lifted Little Squirrel onto his shoulders.

"Let's play together," he said. "Let's run!"

Little Squirrel held on tightly as they whooshed through the woods.

"Yippee!" he shouted.

"Let's climb!" said Daddy Squirrel. Little Squirrel kept his eyes open wide as they reached the top of a tree.

"Wheeee!" he shouted.

"And now," said Daddy Squirrel, "let's jump!"

SPLAT!

"Oh, help!" cried Daddy Squirrel. "Now I'm stuck!"

Little Squirrel giggled as he helped his daddy out of the sticky mud.

"You can do everything, Little Squirrel!" said Daddy proudly. "You can even save a Daddy Squirrel!"

Little Squirrel grinned. "I love playing with you… and I love my daddy!" he shouted, and they raced home happily together.

The Ant and the Dove

One morning, a thirsty ant went down to the river for a drink. Suddenly…SWOOSH! A ripple swept the tiny ant off the riverbank and into the water.

"Help!" cried the ant.

A kind dove heard the ant's cries. She swooped down and dropped a leaf into the water near him.

"Climb onto this," she cooed.

"Oh, thank you," gasped the ant. "You saved my life!" And he floated back to the shore on the leaf.

A little later, the ant was drying off in the sun when he saw a hunter trying to catch the dove with a net.

The ant wanted to help his new friend, so he scurried over to the hunter and bit his foot.

"Ouch!" yelled the hunter.

Startled by the noise, the dove flew away.

"Thank you," she called out to the ant. "Now you've saved my life, too!"

And the moral of the story is: one good turn deserves another.

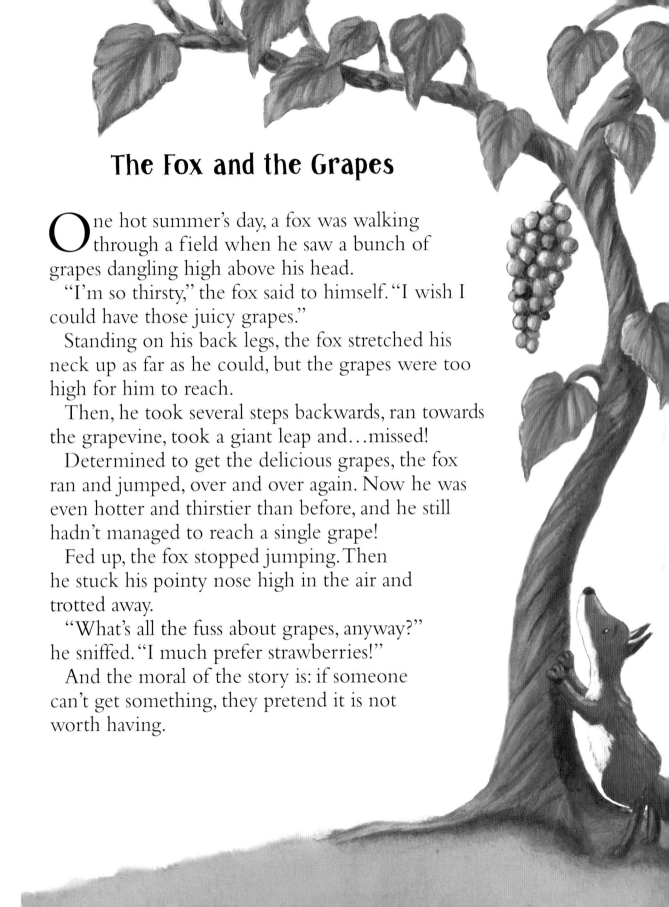

The Fox and the Grapes

One hot summer's day, a fox was walking through a field when he saw a bunch of grapes dangling high above his head.

"I'm so thirsty," the fox said to himself. "I wish I could have those juicy grapes."

Standing on his back legs, the fox stretched his neck up as far as he could, but the grapes were too high for him to reach.

Then, he took several steps backwards, ran towards the grapevine, took a giant leap and…missed!

Determined to get the delicious grapes, the fox ran and jumped, over and over again. Now he was even hotter and thirstier than before, and he still hadn't managed to reach a single grape!

Fed up, the fox stopped jumping. Then he stuck his pointy nose high in the air and trotted away.

"What's all the fuss about grapes, anyway?" he sniffed. "I much prefer strawberries!"

And the moral of the story is: if someone can't get something, they pretend it is not worth having.

The Man from the Moon

Most people think that the moon is empty. It certainly looks empty. But there's a man who lives there who is very clever, and he knows how to hide.

Every night, the man from the moon puts on his space suit, steps into his candy-striped rocket and zooms off into space to explore the planets. But you never see him because he always takes off from the other side of the moon.

"I love space!" said the man from the moon one night, as he shot past stars and planets. "Get ready for an adventure, little rocket. Tonight, we're going to visit a new world!"

They landed on a very strange planet. It was covered in forests of bendy trees.

The man from the moon climbed the trees and played with some purple aliens who lived in them. He swung from the branches by his toes and waved to everyone he saw.

"This is the best planet ever!" he said. "I wish there was somewhere like this on the moon!"

The purple aliens were very curious about the rocket. They climbed on it and peered into it and patted it. And while the man from the moon was looking the other way, the bravest alien of all crept inside and hid under the seat.

When it was time to leave, the aliens gave the man from the moon some snacks for his journey. He waved goodbye and blasted off in his candy-striped rocket. But halfway home, the stowaway alien crawled out from under his seat! A big, beaming smile spread across the face of the man from the moon.

"There's going to be a little bit of the forest on the moon after all!" he cheered.

Most people think that the moon is empty. But the man who lives there is very clever at hiding himself…and so is his new alien friend!

113

Grandmother Cedar Tree

Once, there lived a large grandmother cedar tree called Seedla. She was tall and strong, but she was sad and lonely.

The Sky God felt sorry for Seedla. He told the warm and gentle South Wind to plant a baby cedar tree next to the grandmother tree.

Seedla was overjoyed and she adopted the baby cedar tree as her grandson.

As the little tree grew, he sprouted fresh, tender branches. Soon, animals came to nibble on them, and the little tree struggled to grow bigger.

So Seedla moved her long, old branches back and forth to scare the animals away. And the little tree began to grow taller and stronger.

Sometimes, when the cold and wintry North Wind blew extra hard, the little tree felt that his thin branches would bend and break.

So Seedla put her long, strong arms around her grandson to protect him from the North Wind. Then the little tree grew some more.

Sometimes the sun was so strong that it scorched the little tree. So Seedla raised her branches high enough to shade her grandson. And the little tree kept growing.

In time, Seedla's grandson became tall and straight. Many seasons passed. Grandmother Seedla became old and tired. Her grandson, who was now large and strong, felt her sorrow.

"Grandmother, remember when the animals nibbled on me, how you moved your strong branches to protect me?" he said to her. "Well, I have long arms now. I will move them back and forth to scare the animals away like you did.

"And Grandmother, do you not remember when I was small and thin, and the North Wind blew so strongly that I thought I would break, how you put your arms around me to keep me from breaking? My arms are strong now and I can keep you from bending and breaking.

"And Grandmother, remember when the sun scorched my branches, you lifted your branches high to shade me? Well, now I can lift my long arms to shade you.

"As you took care of me, now I will take care of you."

The grandmother tree smiled gratefully at her grandson, and the two stood side by side for many more seasons.

Jungle Ballet

Milly Monkey didn't like the dark. She snuggled up on Granny Monkey's knee and tried not to look at it, but it was all around her.

"The dark isn't scary," said Granny Monkey. "Don't you know what happens at night when the stars come out?"

Milly shook her head.

"Sometimes, the jungle puts on a magical ballet," whispered Granny Monkey. "Little lights twirl and dance, but you can only see them if you're in bed."

Milly longed to see the ballet. Bravely, she climbed into bed and said goodnight. Then Granny Monkey began to sing a beautiful lullaby. Her song called all the fireflies in the jungle and they danced around Milly's head until she fell asleep.

Next day, Milly told Granny Monkey, "You were right. Dark isn't scary. Dark is magical."

And Granny Monkey gave a wise old smile!

Brave Amy

Amy the ostrich wasn't like her ostrich friends. They were afraid of everything – from loud noises to sandstorms. And whenever anything scared them, they buried their heads in the sand. But Amy never did.

Amy dreamed of having adventures, but her friends just laughed.

"Ostriches don't go travelling," they said. "It's much too scary."

One evening, the ostriches heard a big noise drifting across the plain. BANG! BANG! TOOT! TOOT! Of course, they all buried their heads in the sand. But not Amy – she stood up straight.

"I'm not scared," she said bravely.

In the evening light, she saw a travelling band marching towards her. They were playing drums and trumpets. BANG! BANG! TOOT! TOOT! And they all looked very happy.

"I like your band," Amy said shyly.

"Then join us!" said a camel with a drum.

Amy looked at her friends with their heads buried in the sand and she knew what she wanted to do.

Now, Amy has great adventures with the marching band, and she bangs the loudest drum of all!

Tractor Mayhem

It was a beautiful sunny day on Friendship Farm, but Hank Hayseed couldn't enjoy it just yet. He had work to do.

"When you're finished we can have a picnic down by the duck pond," said his wife, Molly. "I'll just pop into town for some groceries."

Hank and his sheepdog Gus watched Molly drive off in her old jeep.

"We'll get the chores done in no time if we use my tractor," said Hank.

Gus wasn't so sure. That tractor was pretty old! And sure enough, the moment Hank started the engine, black smoke came pouring out.

"Oh, bother!" said Hank. "What am I going to do now?"

Then he had a crackerjack idea. Hank pushed the tractor into his workshop, closed the doors and set to work. The farm animals gathered round, trying to peek in and see what he was up to.

"Every time he tries to fix something, he only makes it worse," clucked Mrs Beak.

"Here he comes," said Gus. "Let's skedaddle!"

Hank rode out on his tractor. "Yee-harr!" he hollered, waving his hat like a cowboy at a rodeo.

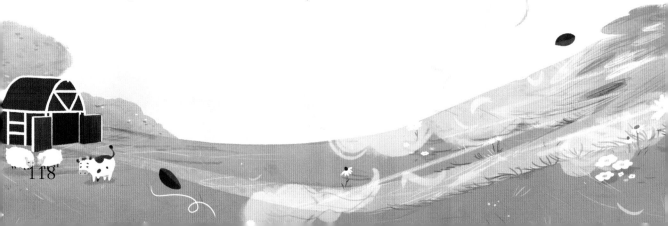

The old tractor looked as good as new. Hank had fixed it up, given it a lick of paint – and fitted rocket boosters!

"With a vehicle like this, we'll be the best farm in the whole county!" Hank said proudly. "Hop aboard, Gus – we've got work to do!"

Hank pulled the lever. Flames shot out of the rocket boosters and the tractor zoomed off!

Bailey the horse saw the tractor roaring towards him carrying hay for his breakfast.

"About time," he neighed. "I'm starving."

Hank pulled the lever to stop the tractor – and that's when everything started to go wrong. Instead of stopping, the tractor went faster! As it shot past, a hay bale flew off the trailer and landed – THUNK! – on Bailey's head.

"Sorry, Bailey!" Hank called back over his shoulder.

Hank wrestled with the pesky lever. But it was no use…and now they were heading for old Maggie the cow.

"The lever's stuck fast!" Hank cried as Gus held on.

"I do believe," said Maggie grandly, "it is rude for anyone to move that fast."

But she moved fast enough herself when she saw the tractor was coming straight for her…and wasn't going to stop!

Up ahead, Mrs Beak and her ducklings were paddling on the pond. As the tractor splashed through the water, a wave sent them flying!

"We've got to stop this thing!" said Hank, grappling with the lever. He gave an almighty tug – and it came off in his hands.

"Jumping jelly beans!" Hank cried. "We're out of control!"

And that's when Molly arrived home.

"Are you okay?" she cried.

"Yes, dear!" Hank called back. "Just taking Wallow a bucket of pig food!"

Hank held up the bucket to show Molly as the tractor whizzed past her. Then they hit a bump and the bucket went flying out of his hands…and landed on Molly's head!

"Hold on tiiiiiiiight!" yelled Hank as the tractor zoomed up the sloping roof of Wallow the pig's sty as if it were a ramp. It shot into the air…and landed slap-bang in the middle of the duck pond!

Hank and Gus were soaked, and Friendship Farm was a terrible mess.

"This'll take all day to fix!" groaned Hank.

"Nonsense!" said Molly, still pulling food scraps from her hair. "We can do it and still have time for a picnic, just as long as we all pitch in and work together!"

And everyone agreed that was a crackerjack idea.

The Gingerbread Man

There was once a little old woman and a little old man. One morning, the little old woman decided to bake a gingerbread man. She mixed all the ingredients together, rolled out the dough, cut out the gingerbread man, then popped him in the oven to bake.

But when the little old woman opened the oven door, the gingerbread man jumped up and ran away.

"Stop!" cried the little old woman.

"We want to eat you!" cried the little old man. And they ran after the gingerbread man. But he was too fast.

"Run, run, as fast as you can. You can't catch me, I'm the gingerbread man!" he sang.

Then he darted into a field, passing a pig, a cow and a horse. They all wanted to eat him, too!

"I've run away from a little old woman and a little old man, and I can run away from you!" he told the animals. And he sang, "Run, run, as fast as you can. You can't catch me, I'm the gingerbread man!"

The little old woman, the little old man, the pig, the cow and the horse ran and ran, but none of them could catch the gingerbread man.

After a while, the gingerbread man reached a river.

"How will I get across?" he cried.

A sly fox saw the gingerbread man, and licked his lips.

"Jump onto my back and I will take you across the river," he told the gingerbread man.

So the gingerbread man jumped onto the fox's back and the fox began to swim across the river.

After a while, the fox cried, "You're too heavy for my back. Jump onto my nose." So the gingerbread man scrambled onto his nose.

But as soon as they reached the riverbank, the fox flipped the gingerbread man up into the air, and he fell straight into his open jaws. The fox snapped his mouth shut and gobbled him up.

And that was the end of the gingerbread man!

The Morning and the Evening Star

Once upon a time, there were two stars who were the sons of the Golden King of the Heavens. The two brothers were called Tschen and Shen. They loved each other very much, but they were always quarrelling.

One evening, they started arguing as usual.

"I shine brighter than you," mocked Shen.

"No you don't!" roared Tschen. "I can twinkle all night!" And he struck Shen a terrible blow.

Both stars were so angry, they made a vow there and then that they would never look upon each other again.

Their father tried to help them make friends, but the brothers would not listen.

So now, Tschen only appears in the evening as the Evening Star. And Shen only appears in the morning as the Morning Star, once Tschen has disappeared from sight.

The two stars never appear together, but their father continues to try to get them to make peace with each other.

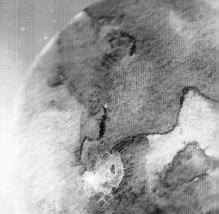

The Moon Lake

A terrible drought came to the jungle, and the elephants' watering hole dried up. They travelled to another lake on the other side of the jungle. On the way, they passed through a colony of rabbits. Hundreds of rabbits were injured under the herd's big stomping feet.

"We must stop the elephants passing through here again," shouted the rabbit king, and he went to ask the elephant king to meet him at the lake.

There, the two kings saw the moon reflected in the still water.

"I have a message from the moon," said the rabbit king. "You have soiled his lake. You must leave, or something terrible will happen to your herd."

"I'm so sorry," cried the elephant king. As he bowed down, his trunk rippled the water. The moon seemed to move.

"Now the moon is angrier than ever," said the rabbit king. "You have touched the sacred water of his lake."

"Oh, please forgive me!" wept the elephant king. "We will never come here again." And the elephants went away. It never occurred to them that the clever little rabbit had tricked them!

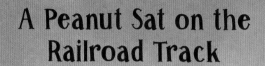

A Peanut Sat on the Railroad Track

A peanut sat on the railroad track,
His heart was all a-flutter;
Along came a train – the 9:15 –
Toot, toot, peanut butter!

The Man in the Moon

The man in the moon
Came tumbling down,
And asked his way to Norwich.
He went by the south,
And burned his mouth
With supping cold pease-porridge.

Curly Locks

Curly Locks! Curly Locks! Wilt thou be mine?
Thou shalt not wash dishes, nor yet feed the swine,
But sit on a cushion and sew a fine seam,
And feed upon strawberries, sugar and cream!

Michael Finnegan

There was an old man called Michael Finnegan
He grew whiskers on his chinnegan
The wind came out and blew them in again
Poor old Michael Finnegan. *Begin again…*

Old Betty Blue

Old Betty Blue
Lost a holiday shoe.
What can old Betty do?
Give her another
To match the other,
And then she may swagger in two.

Little Nancy Etticoat

Little Nancy Etticoat, in a white petticoat,
And a red rose.
The longer she stands,
The shorter she grows.

What is she? A candle!

127

Sleeping Beauty

Once upon a time, a king and queen had a beautiful baby girl. The proud parents decided to hold a christening feast to celebrate, so they invited kings, queens, princes and princesses from other kingdoms.

Five good fairies lived in the kingdom and the king wanted them to be godmothers to his daughter. One of these fairies was very old and no one had seen her in years, or even knew where she was. So when the king sent out the invitations, he invited only the four young fairies.

The day of the christening arrived, and the palace was full of laughter and dancing.

After the delicious feast, the four fairies gave the princess their magical gifts.

The first fairy waved her wand over the crib and said, "You shall be kind and considerate."

The second fairy said, "You shall be beautiful and loving."

The third fairy said, "You shall be clever and thoughtful."

Suddenly, the palace doors flew open. It was the old fairy. She was furious because she hadn't been invited to the feast.

She flew up to the crib and waved her wand over the princess.

"One day, the king's daughter shall prick her finger on a spindle and fall down dead!" she screeched, and then rushed out.

"I cannot undo the spell," said the fourth fairy, "but I can soften it. The princess will prick her finger on a spindle, but she will not die. Instead, the princess, and everyone within the palace and its grounds, will fall into a deep sleep for a hundred years."

The king thanked the fairy and then, to protect his daughter, ordered every spindle in the kingdom to be burned.

The years passed, and the princess grew into a beautiful, clever and kind young woman.

One day, the princess decided to explore some rooms in the palace that she had never visited before. After a while, she came to a little door at the top of a tall tower. Inside, there was an old woman working at her spinning wheel. The princess didn't know that the woman was really the old fairy in disguise.

"What are you doing?" the princess asked curiously.

"I'm spinning thread, dear," replied the woman.

"Can I try?" asked the princess.

No sooner had she touched the spindle than she pricked her finger and fell into a deep sleep.

As she fell asleep, every living thing within the castle walls fell into a deep sleep too.

As time passed, a hedge of thorns sprang up around the palace. It grew higher and thicker every year, until only the tallest towers could be seen above it.

The story of the beautiful princess who lay sleeping within its walls spread throughout the land. She became known as Sleeping Beauty. Many princes tried to break through the thorns to rescue Sleeping Beauty, but none were successful.

Exactly a hundred years after the princess had fallen asleep, a handsome prince, having heard the story of Sleeping Beauty, decided to try to awaken the sleeping princess.

The prince didn't know that the fairy's spell was coming to its end. As he pushed against the thick hedge, every thorn turned into a beautiful rose and a magic path formed to let him pass.

Soon, the prince came to the palace. He saw people and animals asleep in every room.

At last, he found the tiny room in the tower where Sleeping Beauty lay. He kissed her gently.

The sleeping princess opened her eyes and smiled. With that one look, they fell in love.

All around the palace, people started waking up. The spell had been broken!

The king called for a huge wedding feast to be prepared, and this time he invited every person, and fairy, in the entire kingdom.

Sleeping Beauty married her handsome prince and they lived happily ever after.

Roly and Poly

Roly and Poly were polar bears. They lived in the cold, frozen north where they liked to play in the ice and the snow all day long.

One morning, the little bears started to feel tired.

"Let's sit down for a rest!" sighed Roly.

Poly pointed to a big, grey rock sticking out of the sea. "That looks like a brilliant place to sit!" he said.

So Roly and Poly jumped onto the big, grey shape, and settled down for a rest. They yawned and stretched and in no time at all fell fast asleep.

The sky grew dark and the stars began to twinkle. As the little bears snored gently, and the big, silvery moon rose high in the sky, the grey rock suddenly started to move, slipping out into the cold sea.

In fact, the grey rock was not a rock at all. It was a humpback whale, who had just woken up and had no idea that two little bears were fast asleep on her back. The whale dived down into the murky depths, and icy-cold water rushed up around her.

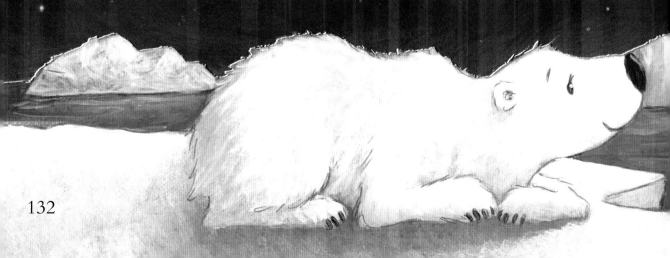

"Yeow!" yelled Roly and Poly, waking up in the sea.

The whale heard the bears' loud cries and came back up to the surface.

"What are you doing out here in the night?" she asked.

"We don't know!" said Roly and Poly together, and they started to cry.

"Well, I'd better take you home," said the whale kindly. "Climb on."

"Your back looks like the grey rock that we sat on," said Roly.

"I think your back *is* the grey rock that we sat on," said Poly.

Roly and Poly enjoyed their moonlight ride, and before long they were home again, safe with their mum. The whale swam off, waving goodbye with her huge tail.

"Goodbye and goodnight!" sighed Roly and Poly, as they drifted off to sleep, dreaming of their big adventure.

The Boy Who Cried Wolf

Once there was a boy called Peter who lived in a little village in the mountains with his parents, who were sheep farmers. It was Peter's job to watch over the flock and protect the sheep from wolves.

Every day, Peter sat on the mountainside watching the flock. It was very quiet with no one but sheep for company. No wolves ever came to eat the sheep.

"Oh, I wish something exciting would happen," groaned Peter. "I'm so bored!"

Finally, one day, Peter couldn't stand it any more. He started shouting at the top of his voice:

"WOLF! HELP! WOLF!"

Down in the village, a man heard Peter's cries.

"Quick!" he shouted. "There's a wolf attacking the sheep."

The villagers grabbed their axes, forks and shovels and ran up the mountain to where Peter was shepherding his flock.

When they got there, the sheep were grazing peacefully.

"Where's the wolf?" one of the villagers cried.

Peter roared with laughter. "There's no wolf. I was just playing!"

The villagers were very angry. "You mustn't cry wolf when there isn't one," they said.

That night Peter got a telling-off from his mother and was sent to bed without any supper.

For a while after this, Peter managed to behave himself, and the villagers soon forgot about his trick.

Then one day, Peter was bored again. Laughing, he picked up some sticks and started banging them hard together. Then at the top of his voice, he shouted, "WOLF! Help! WOLF! There's a big wolf eating the sheep!"

Down in the village, a crowd of people started gathering when they heard the loud banging and shouting.

"It's Peter," someone cried. "Quick, there must be a wolf on the prowl."

Once again, the villagers grabbed their brooms, forks and shovels. They ran up the mountain to chase away the wolf and save poor Peter and his sheep.

And once again, when they got there, the sheep were grazing peacefully.

"Peter, what's happened?" shouted one man angrily.

"There's no wolf," laughed Peter. "I was only playing."

"You shouldn't do that," said another man. "It's not good to lie."

That night, Peter got an even bigger telling-off from his mother and once again had to go to bed without any supper.

Peter decided that he would really try to behave himself from now on, and soon the incident was forgotten.

A few weeks later, while Peter stood counting the sheep to pass the time, he noticed that some of them were bleating nervously.

He climbed up a tree to see what was upsetting them.

To his horror, he saw a big wolf creeping through the grass towards the flock.

Shaking with fear, he started screaming, "WOLF! Help! WOLF! Please hurry, there's a big wolf about to eat the sheep!"

A few people down in the village heard his cries for help, but they carried on about their business as usual.

"It's only Peter playing another trick," they said to each other. "Does he think he can fool us again?"

And so nobody went to Peter's rescue.

By nightfall, when Peter hadn't returned, his parents became concerned. Peter never missed his supper – something bad must have happened.

The villagers hurried up the mountain, carrying flaming torches to light their way.

A terrible sight met their eyes. All the sheep were gone! There really had been a wolf this time.

Peter was still in the tree, shaking and crying.

"I cried out wolf! Why didn't you come?" he wept.

"Nobody believes a liar, even when he's speaking the truth," said Peter's father, helping him climb out of the tree. Peter hung on to his father all the way home. He never wanted to see another wolf ever again.

And Peter finally really learned his lesson. He never told a lie again, and he always got to eat his supper.

Snow White

Once there was a queen who longed for a daughter. As she sat sewing by her window one winter's day, she pricked her finger on the needle. As blood fell from her finger, she thought, "I wish I had a daughter with lips as red as blood, hair as black as ebony wood and skin as white as the snow outside!"

Before long, the queen gave birth to a baby girl with blood-red lips, ebony hair and skin as white as snow. The queen called her daughter Snow White.

Sadly, the queen died and the king married again. His new wife was beautiful, but vain.

She had a magic mirror, and every day she looked into it and asked:

"Mirror, mirror, on the wall,
Who is the fairest of them all?"

Every day, the mirror replied:

"You, O Queen, are the fairest of them all."

But Snow White became more and more beautiful every day. One morning, when the queen asked the mirror who was the fairest, the mirror replied:

"You, O Queen, are fair, it's true.
But young Snow White is fairer than you."

Furious, the queen told her huntsman, "Take Snow White into the forest and kill her!"

The huntsman led Snow White deep into the forest, but he could not bear to hurt her. "Run far away from here," he said.

As darkness fell, Snow White came upon a little cottage. She knocked softly on the door, but there was no answer, so she let herself in. Inside, Snow White found a table and seven tiny chairs.

Upstairs, there were seven little beds.

Snow White lay down on the seventh bed and fell fast asleep.

She awoke to find seven little men staring at her in amazement.

"Who are you?" she asked.

"We are the seven dwarves who live here," said one dwarf. "Who are you?"

"I am Snow White," she replied, and she told them her sad story.

"You can stay with us," said the eldest dwarf, kindly.

Every day, the seven dwarves went to work while Snow White cooked and cleaned the cottage.

"Don't open the door to anyone," they told her, worried the wicked queen might find her.

Meanwhile, when the wicked queen asked her mirror once more who was the fairest that day, it replied:

"You, O Queen, are fair, it's true,
But Snow White is still fairer than you.
Deep in the forest with seven little men
Snow White is living in a cosy den."

The queen was furious and vowed to kill Snow White herself. So she added poison to a juicy apple and set off to the forest, disguised as a pedlar woman.

"Try my juicy apples!" she called out, knocking on the door of the seven dwarves' cottage.

Snow White remembered the dwarves' warning, so she opened only the window to take a look.

When the queen offered Snow White an apple, she took a big bite. The poisoned piece got stuck in her throat and she fell to the ground.

When the seven dwarves returned, they were heartbroken to find their beloved Snow White dead. They couldn't bear to bury her, so they put her in a glass coffin and placed it in the forest, where they took turns watching over her.

One day, a prince rode by and saw Snow White. The dwarves told him her sad story.

"Please let me take her away," begged the prince. The dwarves could see he loved Snow White and they agreed to let her go.

As the prince's servants lifted the coffin, one of them stumbled, jolting the poisoned apple from Snow White's throat, and she came back to life.

When Snow White saw the handsome prince, she fell deeply in love with him.

They soon married and lived happily ever after, together with the dwarves.

Dinosaur Attack!

Felix the dinosaur was the smallest dinosaur in his herd, but there was one thing he could do better than all the others. He could run very, very fast.

"Felix, slow down!" the other dinosaurs said to him every day as he whizzed past.

But Felix wouldn't listen.

One day, the dinosaurs were munching leaves in their camp when they heard a loud THUMP! THUMP!

"It's T. rex!" the chief dinosaur shouted. "Hide!"

All the dinosaurs did exactly as they were told…all except Felix, who had an idea. There was a cliff nearby, and at the bottom was a large lake. If T. rex chased after him, perhaps Felix could lead him off the cliff!

THUMP! THUMP! THUMP! T. rex stomped into the camp. Felix took a deep breath and jumped out in front of him.

"Silly old T. rex!" he shouted, and blew a loud raspberry.

T. rex bared his teeth.

"No one blows raspberries at me!" he roared,
and he started to chase Felix.

Felix ran faster than he had ever run before, all the way to
the cliff – and T. rex got closer and closer.

Just before Felix reached the edge, he grabbed hold of a bush
and stopped sharp. But T. rex was too big to stop himself in time,
and he ran straight off the cliff and landed in the lake.

SPLASH!

"Good riddance!" said Felix, peering over at T. rex spluttering
in the lake below.

All the other dinosaurs in the herd slowly came out of their
hiding places.

"Felix, you're a hero!" said the chief.

"No, I'm not," said Felix in a modest voice. "I'm just a very
fast runner."

"Well, we're very proud of you!" the chief said. "And we'll
never complain about you running again!"

Wherever You Go...I Go

The sun comes up and smiles on us
And starts to warm the early day.
My sleepy eyes can see you move.
Wherever you go...I go.

Then out we dash, to leap and play
And scramble in the morning sun.
You push some leaves aside for me...

(Hey Mum! Hey, look!
Guess who's a tree?!)
Let's go have fun, and mess about.
Whenever you play...I play.

(Oh no!)
The skies turn grey,
It starts to rain
And you just want to keep me dry...
(Thanks Mum!)
I run and shelter under you.
Wherever you are...I am.

And as we walk on, trunk in trunk
And talk about the things I'll do...
(You'll teach me, Mum...
you always do.)
You tell me just how much you care,
(I love you Mum, I sing to you!)
Whatever you love...I love.

Then when it's time to scrub me clean,
We'll splish and splosh and splash about.
You wash away my bathtime fears,
(Just don't forget behind my ears!)
Whenever you smile...I smile.

And when the day has reached its end
And both of us are getting tired,
I'll snuggle up and feel your warmth.
Whenever you sleep...I sleep.

Welcome to the Jungle

Jasper the monkey lived deep in the jungle with his mum, dad and lots of uncles and aunts. When Jasper wasn't busy playing with the other monkeys, he loved exploring the jungle and making new friends.

One day something very exciting happened. Jasper's mum gave birth to a baby boy, called Charlie. Jasper was very excited. He couldn't wait to show his new brother the jungle and introduce him to all his friends.

"Can I take Charlie exploring?" Jasper asked his mum.

"As long as you take good care of him," replied Mum. "And you'll have to carry him – he's much too small to walk very far."

"No problem," laughed Jasper. And he picked up Charlie and began to carry him through the jungle. They had only got as far as the river when Jasper began to puff and pant. Charlie wriggled and screeched with glee. Jasper panted even harder. Charlie was heavier than he'd thought.

"Oh, dear," sighed Jasper. "I don't think I'm going to be able to carry you very far, after all. I think we'll have to go home."

Jasper put Charlie down and sat down on the riverbank. Jasper felt very sad. He had been looking forward to introducing Charlie to all his friends. As he stared into the river, a pair of eyes and two nostrils popped out of the water. Then a crocodile with huge teeth rose to the surface.

Charlie jumped back in fright.

"Don't worry," laughed Jasper. "It's only Cressida the Crocodile." He turned to the crocodile and smiled.

"Hi, Cressida," he called. "Come and meet Charlie, my baby brother. I was going to take him around the jungle to meet everyone, but he's too heavy to carry."

"I could give you a lift," suggested Cressida. "Jump on my back and I'll take you on a river ride."

"What a great idea," said Jasper. The brothers jumped onto the crocodile's back and were soon gliding through the jungle. Jasper had a wonderful time introducing Charlie to his old friends, and just as much fun making new friends along the way. But both Jasper and Charlie agreed that Cressida was the best friend of all!

The Naughty Little Rabbits

Once upon a time, three naughty little rabbits lived with their mama in a cosy hillside burrow.

One day, Mama said, "You're getting so big! Come and help me make your sleeping corners bigger."

The naughty little rabbits didn't want to help Mama. "We want to play outside!" they cried.

"First, there is work to do," their mama said. But the naughty little rabbits scampered off to the meadow, leaving their poor mama behind.

"I wish we had someone to play with," said the first little rabbit, looking around for some excitement.

"Why don't you play with me?" cried a squirrel. "Just do what I do and we'll have some fun."

Then the squirrel scampered up a tree and started throwing acorns that rained down upon the naughty little rabbits.

"Ow!" cried the little rabbits, and they ran away.

"I wish we had something to eat," said the second little rabbit, growing hungry after all that running.

"Why don't you have lunch with me?" croaked a little frog. "Just do what I do. Close your eyes and put out your tongues and you'll catch a yummy fly."

"Yuck! We don't eat flies!" spluttered the little rabbits, pulling their tongues back in and hopping away.

"I wish we could have a cosy nap," said the third little rabbit, tired after so much hopping around.

Before they could curl up, it started to rain. The little rabbits didn't like the rain, and they ran until they reached home.

"We're so sorry, Mama!" cried the little rabbits, as she hugged them close. "Can we help you with the work now?"

"There will be plenty of work for you to do another day," said their mama. "Come and eat your supper, and promise me you won't run off again."

The hungry, sleepy little rabbits ate their supper. Then they crawled into their sleeping corners.

And guess what? Someone had made each one a little bit bigger. Now, who do you think had done that?

Poorly Bunny

Bunny did not feel well. Her little twitchy nose felt all snuffly. "ATISHOO!" she sneezed loudly.

"Oh, my poor little bunny," said her mummy. "I think you've caught a cold."

So Mummy gently tucked Bunny up in bed.

"You need to rest and stay warm," she told her.

"But I don't want to!" sniffled Bunny. "I want to go outside and play!"

Mummy wiped Bunny's sneezy nose and kissed her softly on her fluffy ears.

"Snuggle under your covers and go to sleep now. I'll come and check on you in a little while," she said, as she quietly closed the bedroom door.

But as soon as Mummy had gone, Bunny got out of bed. Her legs felt wobbly and her body ached.

"Come on, Teddy, let's go!" she told her cuddly toy. "We're going outside!"

Shaking and shivering, Bunny slowly crawled downstairs. She was just reaching for the front door handle when Mummy suddenly appeared behind her.

"Bunny!" Mummy scolded. "Where are you going?"

Then Mummy scooped Bunny up into her warm arms and carried her into the lounge.

"Let's snuggle up on the sofa and I'll read you a story," she said softly. "Then, if you feel a bit better, you can go outside."

Bunny smiled and hugged her mummy tightly.

"Thank you," she sighed.

But as Mummy started to read Bunny's favourite book, Bunny's eyes began to feel heavy, and her ears flopped forward.

It was warm and cosy next to Mummy and before long, Bunny was fast asleep.

"Sweet dreams, my little one," Mummy whispered, and she gently carried Bunny back to her bed.

Rumpelstiltskin

Long ago, a poor miller was so desperate to impress the king that he told him his daughter could spin straw into gold!

"This I must see," said the king.

The next day, at the palace, the king led the girl to a room filled with straw.

"Spin this into gold by morning," he demanded, then left.

The girl wept at the impossible task. Suddenly, a strange little man appeared.

"Give me your necklace and I will help you," he told her.

The girl handed it to him, and the strange little man sat in front of the spinning wheel and spun the straw into gold.

The next day, the delighted king took the miller's daughter to an even bigger room filled with straw.

"Spin this into gold and you shall be my queen!" he said.

The strange little man appeared once more, but the girl had nothing left to give him.

"If you become queen," he told her, "you can give me your first-born child."

The girl agreed. Once again, he spun the straw into gold.

The next day, the king married the miller's daughter, and the new queen soon forgot all about the strange little man.

A year passed and the queen had a bonny baby boy. It did not take long for the little man to appear again.

"Please don't take my son," the queen begged.

"If you guess my name, you can keep your baby. You have three days," said the little man.

For two nights after that, the little man appeared in the baby's nursery. The queen tried to guess his name, but all of her guesses were wrong.

On the morning of the third day, one of the queen's servants was in the forest chopping logs when he saw a funny little man leaping around a fire and singing. The servant hid behind a tree and listened:

> *"The queen will never win my game,*
> *For Rumpelstiltskin is my name!"*

The servant hurried home to tell the queen.

That night, when the queen correctly guessed the little man's name, he was furious. He turned red with rage and ran off into the forest, never to be seen again.

Tiny Bear

Tiny Bear was a very curious bear, who was always asking lots of questions: "Why is the sky blue?" "Where does the night go?" "How do worms wiggle?"

"Goodness!" Daddy would laugh. "So many questions!" But, of course, he and Mummy Bear always did their best to give Tiny Bear an answer. Knowing the right answer wasn't always easy, though.

One day, the Bear family was strolling through the forest when Tiny Bear had a funny thought.

"What does the world look like upside down?" he asked.

Mummy and Daddy Bear looked at each other and smiled.

"I can't really tell you!" laughed Mummy Bear. "You are going to have to answer that question for yourself!"

"But how?" asked Tiny Bear.

"I'll show you as soon as we get home," replied Mummy Bear.

Tiny Bear ran home as fast as he could. "Hurry up," he cried. "I want to know what the world looks like upside down."

"Right," panted Mummy Bear. "Stand up straight and stretch your arms up above your head."

"What's that got to do with what the world looks like upside down?" laughed Tiny Bear.

"You'll see in a minute," smiled Mummy Bear. "Point your right foot in front of you, and fall forwards until your hands touch the ground. Then kick your legs into the air and try to hold your legs up straight."

"But I'll fall," squealed Tiny Bear.

"Don't worry," said Mummy Bear. "I'll hold your legs."

Tiny Bear did as Mummy Bear instructed, and could soon do a handstand all by himself.

"What does the world looks like now?" asked Mummy Bear.

"All topsy turvy," laughed Tiny Bear. "This is fun! Why don't you do a handstand and see for yourself?"

"All right," laughed Mummy Bear. "But Daddy Bear will have to do one, too."

Goodnight, Little One

It had been a busy day on Blue Lake Farm. When the sun set and the moon came out, all the animals were ready for their beds. The stars twinkled, and everyone closed their eyes and fell asleep. Everyone, that is, except for Molly's kittens.

Molly had five kittens called Squeaker, Crumble, Ginger, Biscuit and Titch. Each one of them was full to the brim with mischief and fun.

"It's time for bed," said Molly. "Come into the barn and snuggle up on the hay."

But the kittens started leaping between the hay bales to see who could jump the furthest. They tumbled and giggled and jumped. They meowed and bounced and hid. The one thing they didn't do was snuggle up and go to sleep.

Suddenly, Molly had an idea.

"All right," she said. "You can stay up all night long and play as much as you like, on one condition. You are not allowed to fall asleep! No yawning or rubbing your eyes. No catnapping in the corner. Stay awake and play to your hearts' content."

"Hurray!" cheered the kittens. Molly sat in the doorway of the barn to watch them. Squeaker and Biscuit darted into the grass outside the barn and started jumping on each other.

"We're frogs!" Squeaker panted. "Boing! Boing! No one can jump higher than me!"

Crumble and Ginger leaped onto the farm fence and ran up and down like tightrope walkers, springing over each other and keeping their balance perfectly.

Titch scrambled onto the farm roof and sat beside the weathervane, meowing at the moon in his loudest outside voice. Molly put her paws over her ears and hoped that the farmer wouldn't wake up.

Next, all five kittens raced over to the farm's small pond. They played chase, running in circles around the water until they were all so dizzy that they couldn't walk straight. Crumble suddenly gave a big yawn.

"No yawning!" Molly called to him. "You must stay awake."

The kittens ran back over to the barn, but Molly noticed that they weren't quite as bouncy or as loud as they had been before.

"I'm just going to have a little sit down for a minute," said Crumble. He leaned against Molly and his eyes closed. Molly gave a smile.

The other four kittens started to chase some mice. The mice ran through the pigsty, around the chicken coop, through the cow shed and into the meadows. On the way back to the barn, Biscuit and Squeaker kept stopping to sit down and rub their heavy eyes.

"We're just going to sit with you for a minute to warm up," they told Molly. Their eyelids drooped and Molly's smile grew a little wider.

Some birds were swooping around the farmyard. Squeaker started to jump up, trying to knock them out of the air with his paw. But the birds were too quick for him, and soon Squeaker walked over to Molly, panting.

"I'm just going to get my breath back," he said, lying down next to Crumble. He was asleep as soon as he had stopped speaking.

Titch was trying to pounce on his shadow.

"I'm not going to sleep like the others," he said.

Molly smiled at him.

"I love you, Titch."

Titch smiled back, and ran over to give Molly a big cuddle.

"I love you, too," he said. When Molly looked down, she saw that Titch had fallen fast asleep in the middle of the cuddle.

Molly wrapped her tail around all five kittens to keep them safe and warm. Then she closed her eyes and drifted off to sleep in the light of the moon.

I Love My Grandpa

One sunny afternoon, Little Bear went for a walk by the river with Grandpa Bear.

"Shall we have a paddle, Little Bear?"

Little Bear shook his head. "I don't like water, Grandpa," he said.

"Let's just put one paw in," said Grandpa, "and see what it feels like."

Grandpa Bear put one paw in the water.

"Ah!" he said. "That feels good!"

Little Bear put only the tip of his paw in. Then he giggled.

"The water tickles!" he said, and he put the rest of his paw in and waved it about. "Wheeee!"

Grandpa Bear put two paws in. So did Little Bear.

Then Little Bear put all four of his little paws into the cool water.

"Well done, Little Bear!" said Grandpa. "You're paddling! Now, are you ready to make a splash?"

Little Bear kicked his feet, making splashes with a swoosh-swoosh-swoosh! Then suddenly…

SPLOOSH!

In jumped Grandpa Bear, making a gigantic splash!

"Yippee!" cried Little Bear.

"Shall we have a swim now, Little Bear?" said Grandpa Bear.

Little Bear shook his head. "I can't swim, Grandpa!" he said.

"Let's just float," said Grandpa, "and see what it feels like. I will hold you." When Little Bear felt his grandpa holding him, he lifted up one paw at a time, until…

"You're floating!" said Grandpa Bear. "Now, how about some more splashing?"

Little Bear kicked his feet, making more swoosh-swooshes! And suddenly…

"You're swimming, Little Bear!" said Grandpa.

Little Bear swam around and around his grandpa.

"You're the best little swimmer there is," said Grandpa Bear proudly.

When it was time to get out, Grandpa Bear helped Little Bear climb out of the water. Then they both wriggled and jiggled to get dry, spraying water all about.

Grandpa Bear gave Little Bear a warming hug.

"Do you like water now, Little Bear?" he asked, smiling.

Little Bear grinned. "I love water!" he shouted happily. "And…I love my grandpa!"

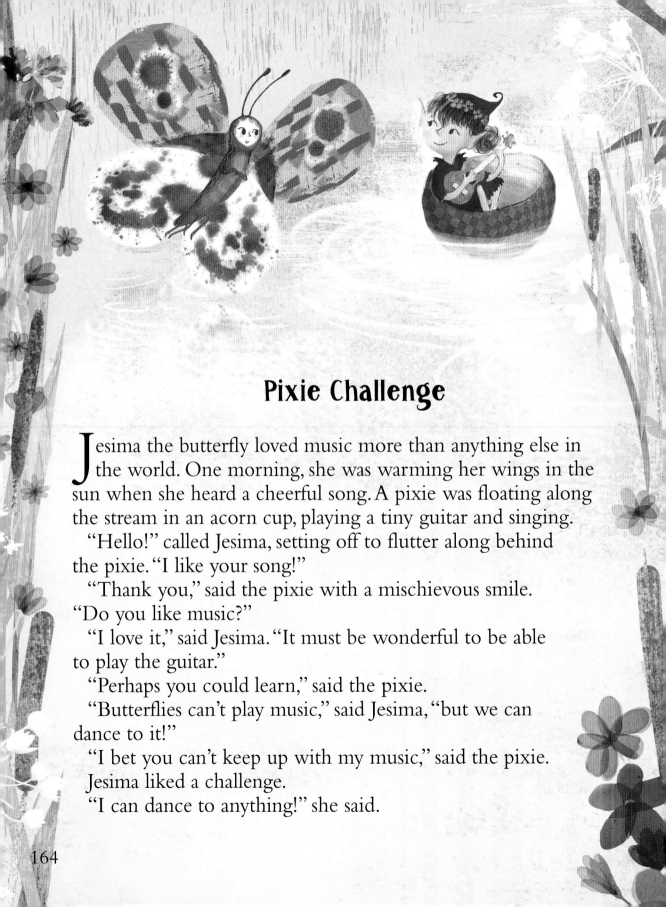

Pixie Challenge

Jesima the butterfly loved music more than anything else in the world. One morning, she was warming her wings in the sun when she heard a cheerful song. A pixie was floating along the stream in an acorn cup, playing a tiny guitar and singing.

"Hello!" called Jesima, setting off to flutter along behind the pixie. "I like your song!"

"Thank you," said the pixie with a mischievous smile. "Do you like music?"

"I love it," said Jesima. "It must be wonderful to be able to play the guitar."

"Perhaps you could learn," said the pixie.

"Butterflies can't play music," said Jesima, "but we can dance to it!"

"I bet you can't keep up with my music," said the pixie.

Jesima liked a challenge.

"I can dance to anything!" she said.

She started to flap her wings in time with the music. But gradually the music grew faster…and faster…and faster! Jesima twirled and flapped her wings even more, but she was starting to get out of breath. Soon the music was so fast that she couldn't keep up any longer. She fluttered down to a rock beside the river, panting, and her wings drooped.

The acorn cup bumped alongside the small rock and the pixie jumped out.

"You should never challenge a pixie," she said with a giggle. "But I will make it up to you."

Jesima didn't know what the pixie meant, but she was so tired from dancing she went to sleep. When she woke up, something felt different. Instead of wings, Jesima had arms and legs. She had been transformed into a pixie! Beside her, on the rock, lay a tiny guitar.

Jesima felt a cheeky giggle bubbling up inside her. She couldn't wait to start playing music – as well as a few mischievous pixie tricks of her own!

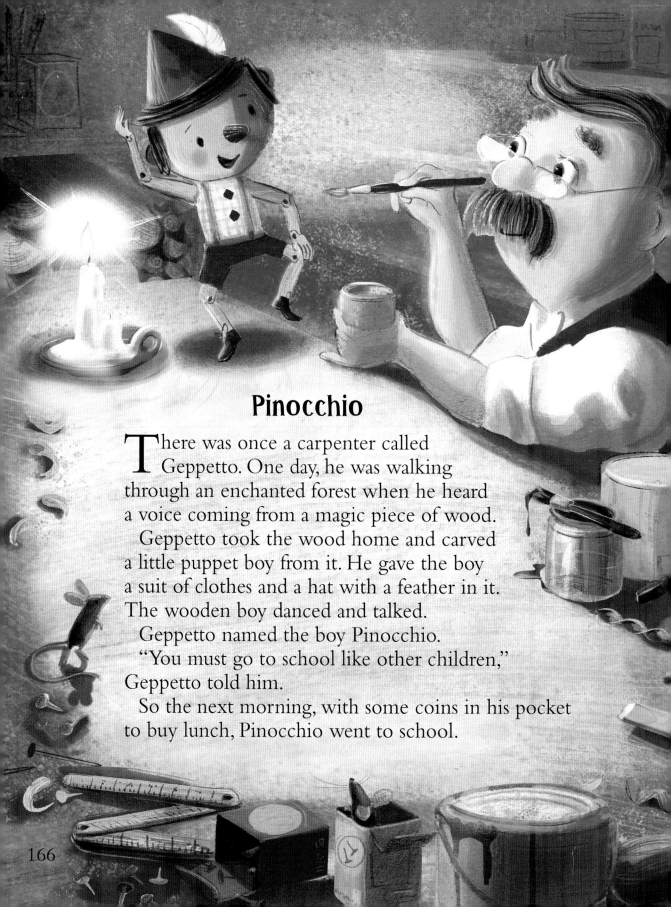

Pinocchio

There was once a carpenter called Geppetto. One day, he was walking through an enchanted forest when he heard a voice coming from a magic piece of wood.

Geppetto took the wood home and carved a little puppet boy from it. He gave the boy a suit of clothes and a hat with a feather in it. The wooden boy danced and talked.

Geppetto named the boy Pinocchio.

"You must go to school like other children," Geppetto told him.

So the next morning, with some coins in his pocket to buy lunch, Pinocchio went to school.

Along the way, a cricket hopped up onto his shoulder.

"You look like you could use a friend," he told Pinocchio. "I will help you learn right from wrong."

Further down the road, Pinocchio met a fox and a cat. They had heard his money jangling in his pocket.

"Come and play with us!" said the fox slyly.

"Pinocchio, you promised your father you would go to school," the cricket whispered.

But Pinocchio, not knowing any better, followed the cat and the fox into a dark forest.

"Plant your money here and it will grow into a money tree," they told Pinocchio. "Just come back tomorrow and you'll see."

The next morning, instead of going to school, Pinocchio went to find his money tree. But when he reached the spot where he'd buried his coins, there was no money tree and his coins had gone.

"They played a trick on you," sighed his friend, the cricket. "They just wanted to get your money."

Pinocchio felt silly, but he pretended he didn't care and stomped off into the forest. The little cricket begged him to go back to Geppetto, but Pinocchio wouldn't listen. Just as it was getting dark, they came to a tiny cottage. Pinocchio knocked on the door loudly and a pretty fairy answered.

"We're lost," explained Pinocchio. "Please can you help us?"

The fairy invited them in and gave them some food.

"Why are you so far from home?" she asked kindly.

Pinocchio didn't want to tell her that he had disobeyed his father.

"I was chased by a giant!" he lied.

Suddenly, Pinocchio's nose grew a little.

"And I ran into the forest to escape!" he continued.

And Pinocchio's nose grew again!

"I have put a spell on you!" said the fairy. "Every time you tell a lie, your wooden nose will grow."

Pinocchio began to cry. "I won't tell any more lies," he promised.

The fairy waved her wand and Pinocchio's nose returned to normal.

"From now on, I will do just as Father tells me," he said. But when he returned home, Geppetto wasn't there. He was out searching for Pinocchio!

"We must find Father and bring him home," he sobbed, feeling bad.

They began their search by the river. But when they got there, Pinocchio fell into the water. The cricket jumped in to help him, but an enormous fish swallowed them both.

There, in the fish's tummy, they found Geppetto! He had been swallowed by the fish too.

Pinocchio hugged his father tightly. "I won't leave you again!" he said.

Then Pinocchio took the feather from his hat and tickled the fish.

"A…a…a…choo!" The fish gave a mighty sneeze, and Geppetto, Pinocchio and the cricket flew out of the fish's mouth and landed on the riverbank.

That night, as Pinocchio slept in his own little bed, the kind fairy flew in through his window.

"You're a good, brave boy," she said, and she kissed him on the forehead.

When Pinocchio awoke the next morning, he found that he was no longer made from wood. He was a real boy! From then on he was always a good son to Geppetto and the best of friends with the cricket, who didn't need to tell him right from wrong ever again.

Pride Goes Before a Fall

One day, ten cloth merchants were returning to their village through the forest. Suddenly, three armed robbers jumped out in front of them and ordered the merchants to hand over all their money and possessions. Even though the merchants outnumbered the robbers, the merchants were scared, so, unhappily, they handed everything over.

The robbers were very pleased with themselves and decided to poke fun at the merchants.

"You must dance for us before we will allow you to go!" laughed one of the robbers.

Thinking they had outsmarted the poor merchants, the three robbers sat down to watch the merchants make fools of themselves.

However, there was one merchant who was very clever. Pondering their situation, he quickly hatched a plan. Then, nodding to his fellow merchants, he took the lead in the dance and started to sing a song.

"We are enty men, they are erith men. If each erith man surround eno men, eno man remains!"

Now, traders have a special language so that they can talk to each other without their buyers knowing what they are saying. The robbers didn't know this trade language – they laughed as they thought the merchants were just singing a funny song. But the other merchants knew that 'enty' means ten, 'erith' means three and 'eno' means one. The lead merchant was saying that they were ten men, the robbers only three, and that if they pounced upon each of the robbers, nine of them could hold them down, while the remaining one could tie them up.

And this is what they did!

The robbers were completely taken by surprise. The ten merchants tied up all the robbers and took back their property. When they returned to their village, they amused their friends with the story of the silly robbers!

The Elves and the Shoemaker

There was once a poor shoemaker who lived with his wife. "We only have enough leather to make one more pair of shoes to sell," said the shoemaker.

So he cut out the leather, ready to stitch the next day, then went to bed.

That night, two elves crept into the shop, dressed in rags. They found the leather and set to work.

The next morning, the shoemaker was amazed to find the finest pair of shoes he had ever seen.

A rich gentleman saw the stylish shoes in the shop and tried them on. He was so delighted with the fit that he paid the shoemaker twice the asking price.

"We can buy more leather," the shoemaker told his wife.

That evening, the shoemaker cut out two more pairs of shoes from the leather, then went to bed.

During the night, the two elves crept into the shop again and set to work on the leather.

In the morning, the shoemaker found two pairs of beautiful shoes. He sold them for more money than he had ever thought possible. Now, the shoemaker had enough money to make four new pairs of shoes.

"Who is helping us?" asked the shoemaker's wife.

That night, the shoemaker cut out the new leather, then he and his wife hid and waited.

It wasn't long before the two little elves appeared and set to work on the leather.

"We must repay our little helpers for their kindness," the shoemaker told his wife.

"Let's make them some fine clothes," said his wife.

So they made the elves two little pairs of trousers, two smart coats and two warm, woolly scarves.

That night, the shoemaker and his wife hid again and watched as the elves found their tiny outfits! They quickly dressed, then danced away happily into the night.

The shoemaker and his wife never saw the elves again. But they continued to make fine shoes and were never poor.

Princess Ava and the Big Smile

Princess Ava was a very lively girl. She was always bouncing around and getting into scrapes. But her father wanted her to act more like a princess.

"You need to be more serious," the king told his daughter.

The princess looked at the king's serious face. And then she looked at his downturned mouth. He looked very sad, so she put her arms around him and gave him a kiss.

"It's not me who needs to be more serious," she told the king, "it's you who needs to smile more, Daddy."

Princess Ava showed the king how to dance around the palace gardens and do cartwheels. The king wasn't very good at them, but he kept on trying and, suddenly, his face wasn't quite so serious.

Princess Ava showed the king how to make a kite swoop through the sky like a bird. The king kept getting his string tangled, but his face was looking less serious by the minute.

"Well done, Daddy!" cried Princess Ava. The king's mouth twitched. It started to turn up at the corners. Then he gave Ava the most wonderful smile.

"I had forgotten how much fun it is to do cartwheels and fly kites," he laughed.

"Oh, Daddy, you do look silly!" giggled Princess Ava.

The happy king did a cartwheel and bounced onto his throne. He was going to pass some new laws in his kingdom.

"From now on," said the king, "I decree that everyone must do at least ten cartwheels a day. And everyone in the palace will have one hour off every morning to practise kite flying."

The king gave Princess Ava a beautiful charm necklace.

"This will remind you that everyone needs a little bit of silliness and fun to keep them smiling," he said.

"Oh, Daddy," giggled Princess Ava, "I've always known that!" And she danced out of the palace to play.

The Little Red Hen

There was once a little red hen who lived on a farm with her friends: a sleepy cat, a lazy pig and a stuck-up duck.

One day, the little red hen found some grains of wheat.

"If I plant these," she thought, "they will grow tall and strong and make more wheat!"

She went to see her friends.

"Who will help me plant these grains of wheat?" she asked.

"Not I," mewed the cat.

"Not I," snorted the pig.

"Not I," quacked the duck.

So the little red hen planted the grains of wheat, and tended to the growing wheat all summer. At last, the wheat was ready to harvest.

"Who will help me harvest the wheat?" the little red hen asked her friends.

"Not I," mewed the cat.

"Not I," snorted the pig.

"Not I," quacked the duck.

So the little red hen harvested the wheat, then went back to her friends.

"Who will help me carry the harvested wheat to the mill?" she asked.

"Not I," mewed the cat.

"Not I," snorted the pig.

"Not I," quacked the duck.

So the little red hen carried the heavy sack of wheat to the mill, where the kind miller ground it to flour.

"Who will help me bake a loaf of bread with this flour?" she asked.

"Not I," mewed the cat.

"Not I," snorted the pig.

"Not I," quacked the duck.

So the little red hen baked a loaf of bread all by herself. "Who will help me eat this delicious bread?" the little red hen asked quietly.

"I will!" mewed the cat.

"I will!" snorted the pig.

"I will!" quacked the duck.

"No, you will not!" cried the little red hen. "I did all the work, and no one helped. My chicks and I will eat the loaf!"

And the little red hen and her little chicks ate up every crumb of the hot, fresh bread.

Jade's First Race

It was Jade the green car's first-ever race. She was very excited and she couldn't stop grinning.

"I hope I get a medal!" she cried.

But around the first bend in the track, she saw Ruby the red car with a burst tyre. So Jade stopped to replace it.

Around the next bend, Yasmin the yellow car called for help.

"Need water!" she panted. So Jade gave her some water.

Around the next bend, she saw Ben the blue car.

"I've run out of petrol!" Ben spluttered.

Jade lent him some petrol, and Ben zoomed off.

But after helping all the other cars, Jade finished the race in last place.

"I'll never get a medal now," she sighed, dipping her headlights as the other cars gathered around.

"Jade came last because she stopped to help us," said Ruby.

"She's the real winner," said Yasmin.

"Jade deserves a medal," said Ben. "Three cheers for the kindest car in the race!"

Brown Bear's Bus Ride

Every day a shiny blue bus full of people roared past Brown Bear's home.

"I wish I could ride on the bus," he murmured. "I wonder where it goes."

Then one morning, a bus ticket fluttered onto the grass outside his cave. He picked it up with trembling paws. His dream had come true!

When Brown Bear climbed onto the bus, the driver stalled the engine in shock and the passengers squealed. Brown Bear couldn't understand why everyone looked so scared. But one little girl wasn't afraid.

"Hello," she smiled, slipping her hand into his paw. "I'm Ella."

When the other passengers saw how brave Ella was, they felt silly. They all shook hands with Brown Bear as the bus set off past the farm, through the town and over the bridges. Now he knew where the bus went!

At the end of his ride, Ella kissed him and the passengers hugged him goodbye.

"Come back soon," they said. "This bus is now bear-friendly!"

I Won't Budge!

The animals were hot and bothered. There had been no rain for days and the watering hole was beginning to dry up under the hot African sun.

"Let's take turns cooling down in the water," suggested the antelope, and all the other animals agreed.

But when the hippo took his turn, he refused to come out of the water.

"You're not being fair," shouted the other animals. "We all want a go."

"No way," said the hippo. "It's far too nice in here…I WON'T BUDGE!"

"That's so mean," cried the animals. "Please let us have a turn."

But the selfish hippo just chanted, "I WON'T BUDGE! I WON'T BUDGE!"

As the sun grew hotter, more animals came to the watering hole. Still the hippo wouldn't budge.

Suddenly, a thundering noise boomed across the plains, followed by a huge thirsty elephant heading right for the watering hole!

All the animals fled, including the hippo, as the elephant charged into the water.

SPLASH!

Once the elephant was settled, the other animals returned.

"Now the elephant won't budge," the hippo grunted.

"Well, you did the same to us," huffed the antelope.

The elephant heard this conversation and felt sorry for the sweltering animals. So he had an idea…

"One…two…three…SQUIRT!" trumpeted the elephant.

"Aaaaah!" sighed the animals, as the spray cooled them down.

But the hippo had been left out.

"Hey, can I have some?" he asked.

"No," said the elephant. "Now you know how it feels."

The hippo drooped his head in shame and turned away.

After a few minutes, the huge elephant shouted, "I think you've learned your lesson."

He grinned at the other animals and cried, "One…two…three…SQUIRT!"

"Thank you!" sighed the hippo, as the cool water splashed against his hot skin. "I won't budge from HERE now!"

The Tortoise and the Hare

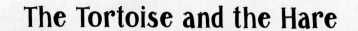

The tortoise and the hare were neighbours. Hare was always in a hurry, while Tortoise was happy to plod along, slowly and steadily.

One day, Tortoise was plodding along the road when Hare sped past him.

"You're so slow!" Hare called. "How do you ever get to where you're going?"

"I get everywhere I want to go!" Tortoise replied crossly. "I'll challenge you to a race."

"A race?" Hare laughed. "You don't stand a chance."

But they arranged a race for the next day, from an old oak tree all the way to the river, and asked Fox to judge it.

"On your marks…get set…go!" Fox shouted.

Hare sprinted ahead. Tortoise slowly set off.

After a few minutes, Hare could see the river ahead. He stopped. Tortoise was nowhere in sight.

"He won't be here for hours," he laughed. "I'll have a rest."

Soon Hare dozed off.

Back along the path, Tortoise carried on, slow but steady.

After an hour, Hare woke up. He could just see Tortoise plodding towards him.

"He's so slow, he still won't be here for hours," Hare muttered, and went back to sleep.

When Hare woke up again, it was late afternoon. He looked down the road, but couldn't see Tortoise anywhere.

"I'll quickly finish the race, so I can go home," Hare sighed, bored with the race now.

Tortoise was waiting for him by the river.

"I've been here for hours!" cried Tortoise. "You are so slow!"

Hare tried to explain, but Tortoise and Fox wouldn't listen.

"But I'm faster!" Hare complained.

"The rules were simple," Fox said. "Tortoise won."

"The race was to get here first," Tortoise smiled, "not to run fastest. Slow and steady wins the race!"

Ten Little Teddies

Ten little teddies, standing in a line,
One of them went fishing, so then there were nine.
Nine little teddies, marching through a gate,
One stopped to tie his shoe, so then there were eight.

Eight little teddies, floating up in heaven,
One fell down and broke his crown, so then there were seven.
Seven little teddies, doing magic tricks,
One made himself disappear, so then there were six.

Six little teddies, about to take a dive,
One of them was scared of heights, so then there were five.
Five little teddies, running on the shore,
One went surfing in the waves, so then there were four.

Four little teddies, eating cakes for tea,
One of them was feeling sick, so then there were three.
Three little teddies, heading for the zoo,
One thought he'd take the bus, so then there were two.

Two little teddies, playing in the sun,
One of them got sunburned, so then there was one.
One little teddy, who's had lots of fun,
It's time for him to go to sleep, so now there are none.

Midnight Fun

Just as midnight's striking,
When everyone's asleep,
Teddies yawn and stretch and shake,
And out of warm beds creep.

They sneak out from their houses,
And gather in the dark,
Then skip along the empty streets,
Heading for the park.

And there beneath the moonlight,
They tumble down the slides,
They swoosh up high upon the swings,
And play on all the rides.

And when the sun comes peeping,
They rush home to their beds,
And snuggle down as children wake,
To cuddle with their teds!

You're Not My Mum!

Gerry and Mum were walking one day, when a line of termites came marching their way.

Gerry watched as they passed by, one by one...but when he looked up his Mummy was gone!

"Lost your mum?" asked Sunbird. "She's nearby, don't you worry! The termites will show you the way if you hurry."

So off Gerry galloped in great leaps and bounds, till he screeched to a halt by some huge termite mounds.

"Aha!" Gerry cried. "Now I'm on the right trail. That looks like my mum's tufty tail!"

But it was Elephant.

"You're not my mum!" Gerry cried.

"Lost your mum?" smiled Elephant. "Just let me think. Is she down at the riverside having a drink?"

Gerry ran to the river as quick as a flash. There he saw something blinking and heard a loud splash.

"Aha!" Gerry cried. "Now what's that I spy? That sounds like Mum drinking – and look, there's her eye!"

But it was Crocodile.

"You're not my mum!" he cried.

"Lost your mum?" cackled Croc. "Take a look over there. I'm sure I saw something with spotty brown hair."

A little way off, Gerry heard a strange sound – something was snoring nearby on the ground!

"Aha!" Gerry cried, as he peered through a gap. "I'm sure that's my mum! She's just taking a nap!"

But it was Leopard.

"You're not my mum!" cried Gerry.

Leopard yawned as he woke. "There's one place you could try. In that baobab tree I heard something up high."

Near the baobab tree Gerry started to stare. Was there something familiar moving up there?

"Aha!" Gerry cried. "That looks just like Mum's neck, stretching up for some leaves. I'll just go and check!"

But it was Snake.

"You're not my mum!" cried Gerry.

"Lossst your mum?" whispered Snake. "If she loves to chew, there are nice tasssty leaves in that clump of bamboo."

By now Gerry felt like he'd been searching for hours. But at last – what was standing behind those bright flowers?

"Aha!" Gerry cried, and he started to laugh. "Who else could have feet like that but a giraffe?"

But it was Zebra.

"You're not my mum!" cried Gerry.

"Lost your mum?" chuckled Zebra, as he flicked off the flies. "Go back to the woods, and you'll get a surprise."

As Gerry came close to the thick jungle glade,
he saw some giraffes in the cool of the shade.

Then from the trees came a voice, saying...
"Hi, little guy!"

Gerry looked up and cried...
"That's my mum!"

So Gerry and Mum,
in the shade of a tree,
had a big Mummy hug
that was snug as can be.

Jerry's Sandcastle

Jerry the hamster lived beside the sea. From his cage in the window, he watched children building sandcastles and splashing in the water.

"I wish I could play in the sand," he sighed.

Then, one night, Jerry reached through the bars and unlocked his cage. He slipped out and ran all the way to the beach.

"How wonderful!" he said, gazing at the moonlit sea.

As the waves crashed on the shore, he built turrets and battlements, dungeons and towers. He played in his sandcastle all night. Then, he scurried into the sand dunes and fell fast asleep.

When Jerry woke up, the sea had washed his castle away. He looked up at his cage in the window. He missed the warm house and his cosy cage, and decided to go home. Of course, now he could visit the beach whenever he wanted!

"I can build sandcastles every night," he said. "And my next one will be even bigger!"

A Chilly Change

Edward the polar bear and his brother Charlie sold vanilla ice cream. But Edward had big ideas. He wanted to do something special with the ice cream – something different.

"Maybe I should make up some flavours," he said.

"Ice-cream flavours – that's crazy!" said Charlie. "No one will buy them. Vanilla is best and I don't want to change."

"Change is exciting!" said Edward.

"Change is scary," said Charlie.

But Edward wouldn't give up. He thought about all the tastes he loved. Then he started inventing. Fish and iceberg flavour! Eel surprise! Salt and snowberries! Edward invented a new taste every day.

Edward and Charlie started to sell more and more ice cream. The news spread, and soon seals, gulls and Arctic foxes were queuing up to taste the incredible flavours.

"You were right," Charlie laughed, at last. "I'm sorry. Sometimes, change is a very exciting thing indeed!"

A New Home for Bear

Bear lived all alone on a dusty shelf in the playroom. His boy was grown up now and didn't have time for toys any more. Then, one day, the boy took him down and dusted him off.

"I think it's time you found a new home," he smiled. "I'm going to put you on the toy table at the school jumble sale."

Bear was very excited. He couldn't wait to find a new child to love. He sat on the toy table and smiled his best smile. But when a little girl reached over to pick up a china doll, she knocked him over and he fell to the ground.

Soon the jumble sale was over and the toy table was put away. No one noticed poor Bear all alone in the grass.

It grew dark and Bear shivered. But he was a brave teddy bear and wasn't afraid of the dark.

In the morning, the sun came up and shone on the pretty flowers. Bear smiled happily – especially when a little girl came by.

"What a happy bear!" she laughed when she saw him. And she picked him up and took him home. She gave him a bath and a ribbon for his neck. At last, Bear had found a new home.